Praise for *The Collectors*

"*The Collectors* is a compelling portrait both of the way a heated mind can come to recreate the world and of how fascination with such a mind can end up being its own sort of trap. A wonderful, obsessive novella."
—Brian Evenson, author of *Fugue State* and *Last Days*

"Bell's fiction excites pity for those who live, as though walled up, in ruins of their own necessary construction. I admire *The Collectors* for the certainty of its prose and its unflinching observation of a most profound alienation—envying the first; fearing the second; and unhappily aware that artifice—no matter how splendid—is inadequate to ameliorate the despair."
—Norman Lock, author of *Shadowplay*

"Matt Bell's lifesick pair, Langley and Homer, shell-shocked under a pile of newspapers, are disquieting, hilarious, and—in that strange way that makes Beckett's and Kafka's characters so urgent—entirely recognizable. Bell has written a beauty."
—Deb Olin Unferth, author of *Vacation*

"*The Collectors* suggests, ultimately, that there exists no better form of renewal than the accommodating art of story."
—John Domini, *Bookslut*

"Matt Bell's *The Collectors* is a jaw-dropping achievement."
—Adam Robinson, *The Chapbook Review*

Praise for *How the Broken Lead the Blind*

"There is an insistent rhythm in everything Matt Bell writes. Not the thudding hammer blows of fraudulent drama, not the drip of leaking satire, certainly not the jolly click and tap of a story that could be—ought to have been—texted. It's gentle and enormously powerful: the beating of a heart."

—Gary Amdahl, author of *Visigoth* and *I Am Death*

"Throughout the collection, Bell… uses propulsive, almost metrical language—often with skillful short sentences—to create the sense of foreboding and imminent surprise we have come to expect from flash fiction."

—Steven Wingate, *The Short Review*

"Matt Bell can do what so many fiction writers can't: Matt Bell can make anything happen."

—Michael Kimball, author of *Dear Everybody*

HOW THEY WERE FOUND

HOW THEY WERE FOUND

stories by
MATT BELL

keyhole press

Keyhole Press
an imprint of Dzanc Books
www.keyholepress.com

Portions of this book originally appeared in *Caketrain, Conjunctions, Gulf Coast, Hayden's Ferry Review, Keyhole, Meridian, No Colony, PANK, Storyglossia, Wigleaf, Willow Springs,* and *You Must Be This Tall to Ride.* "The Collectors" was originally published as a limited-edition chapbook by Caketrain Press.

Cover design by Steven Seighman.

ISBN: 978-0-9821512-5-9

www.howtheywerefound.com

For Jessica

TABLE OF CONTENTS

And when at last it is over, there is no evidence: no weapon, no blood, and no body. The only clue might be the shadows beneath your eyes or a terribly thin line near the corner of your mouth indicating something has been suffered, that in the privacy of your life you have lost something and the loss is too empty to share.

House of Leaves
Mark Z. Danielewski

THE CARTOGRAPHER'S GIRL

To begin, a key: **O** is the place where the cartographer first met the girl. • is the place where they kissed for the first time. ⊙ is any place he told her he loved her, anywhere she once said it back.

The cartographer wanders the city streets, crosses the invisible boundaries that lie between neighborhoods. He takes notes, studies the geography of streets and sewers, of subway lines and telephone wires. His bag holds nothing of value beyond the tools of his trade: his pens and papers, his sextant, his rulers and stencils, plus his dozens of compasses, some worth a month's rent and others bought in bulk at dollar stores and pawn shops. The compasses are disappointingly true, pointing north over and over, when all he wants is for one to dissent, to demur, to show him the new direction he cannot find on his own.

Even the compasses that break, that learn some new way, none ever point him to her. At least not yet. It is not their fault, but his. He is making the wrong kind of map, knows he is, but can't stop himself. All the maps he's made since she left have been wrong, but the cartographer does not know the kind of map he needs.

Different maps have different requirements, and trying to make the wrong kind of map in the wrong way is an obvious mistake.

Less obvious is how making the right map in the wrong way will also fail completely, with no indication of how close he is to his goal. There is no partial success to hope for. He will either find his way to her or else he won't.

When she started sleepwalking, neither of them knew where she was trying to go or why she was going there. She was an expert at slipping out without him noticing, at opening the bedroom door and then the apartment door without making a noise. He'd awaken and find her missing, and then it would be a mad scramble down the stairs, down the street, trying to figure out where she went.

Sometimes he found her sitting in the lobby of their building, or on a bench a block or two away. On other nights, he'd search for hours, only to return home and find her asleep in their bed, her nightgown streaked with mud.

During her worst episodes, she would be gone for days, days in which he didn't sleep or eat or work, instead wandering the city with someone else's map in his hand, some official version of the city drawn by a company or a commission, an agreed upon fiction with which he hoped to guess where she might have gone.

Afterward, she could never explain where she'd gone or what she'd been feeling while sleepwalking. After the first months, the cartographer realized he wasn't supposed to ask anymore, that she couldn't or wouldn't answer his questions no matter how insistently he pried.

All she'd ever say was, Let's just enjoy the time we have together, and then she'd cling to his body like the mast of a sinking ship, like she had lashed herself to him.

One time, near the end, the cartographer found her in the Broad Street subway station, sitting beside the train tracks, crying into the red scarf she always wore wrapped around her neck. When he asked why she was crying, she told him she had just missed it, that she'd been so close this time. She said the word *skinny* over and over, but he didn't ask what she meant. He'd stopped asking long ago, when she'd begged him to.

Besides, she herself was skinny now, had lost so much weight in the previous months. How was he supposed to know it meant something else entirely?

He'd looked down the empty tracks, into the open mouth of the subway tunnel. He worried she'd hurt herself, that if he didn't stop her she'd do something terrible. Now she was gone, and it was he who was hurt: by her absence, by not knowing where she went, by not knowing a sure way to follow.

❖ is any place where he believed he saw her after her disappearance. It is any place he circles back to, week after week after week.

The cartographer compulsively maps everywhere he visits, draws on any surface he can find. At the bar down the street from his house, he draws topological renditions of the layout of the tables, of the path from his stool to the bathroom, of the distribution of waitresses or couples or smoke. There are many kinds of maps, but none of these get him any closer to where he needs to be. He keeps drawing anyway, keeps drinking too, until he feels his head begin to nod. He pays his tab, gets up to leave. If he walks home fast enough, he might be able to fall asleep without dreaming of her.

It is never enough to assume that the reader of the map will approach it with the same mindset the cartographer does. Even omitting something as simple as a north arrow can render a map useless, can cast doubts on all it's trying to communicate. Other markings are just as necessary. There must be a measurement of scale, and there must be a key so that annotations and markings can be deciphered, made useful.

Even though the map is for only himself, it must still be as perfect as possible.

✠ is any place she woke up after sleepwalking, any place he found her, disoriented and scared. He makes this mark over and over and over and over.

Her sleepwalking: It wasn't the only thing wrong with her, but it wasn't until after she disappeared that he opened his mail to find the first medical bills, sent from hospitals all over the city. She'd been hiding them from him, keeping him safe from how sick she was.

Opening each envelope, he saw the names of procedures she'd undergone, the dollar amounts she owed after the insurance paid its share: Blood tests. X-rays. EEGs, EKGs, acronyms on top of acronyms.

Prescriptions for anti-seizure medications, for sleeping pills in increasingly powerful dosages.

He read *electric shock treatments*, the phrase bringing him near tears the first time he read it, wracking him with gasping cries when he began to see it over and over and over.

The cartographer received dozens of these letters in the months after she left, and it was only then that he realized the full scope of her problems.

Sleepwalking, sure, but this too: She was sick, possibly dying, had been almost as long as he'd known her. And she hadn't wanted him to know.

One of their last dates before her disappearance was to see a show at the planetarium near the park. Hand in hand, they watched black holes bend light, obscuring everything nearby in their greed for photons. They watched supernovas, the death of one star, and they watched a recreation of the Big Bang, the birth of many. He remembers how she leaned in close and whispered that in a universe as mysterious as theirs, anything might be possible, and that it was therefore completely reasonable to believe in miracles.

⌘ is somewhere he thought he'd find her using his map.
⌘ is false hope, easily crushed.

The cartographer smells her when he wakes, smells all her scents at once: vanilla perfume, hazelnut coffee, apple shampoo. Here, she is only a breeze of memory. As soon as he opens his eyes, as soon as he moves his head, she will be gone.

* * *

◆ is anywhere they had a minor fight, ◆ anywhere they had a major one. These are the spots where he regrets, where he goes to say he's sorry when each new map ends in failure.

No matter how hard he tries, the cartographer cannot keep to ground truth, cannot render the streets and landmarks in precise relation to each other. No cartographer can. Rendering a three-dimensional world in a two-dimensional space means that purposeful errors are necessary to complete the drawing. Even worse than the change in perspective, there are lines that must be shifted, moved out of the way so that names can be affixed to symbols, so that this ■ can be distinguished from this one: ■ . So that these identical markings can become specific places instead of generalized symbols. Denoting one (basement apartment E5, where she lived when they met) from another (the third floor walkup 312, her last apartment before they moved in together) requires space on the map, requires the physical world be made to accommodate the twin realms of information and emotion, the layers of symbols and abstractions necessary to represent the inhabitants of these parallel universes.

In even the best maps, all these short distances add up over time, until the city depicted is hundreds of meters wider than it should be. This is the second way he loses her, the way he feels her slipping away. He fights for accuracy by creating new symbols and more complex keys, each designed to end his reliance on language, on descriptions now unnecessary, obsolete. He saves his words, stockpiles them for the day he and his girl will be reunited, when his map will lead him to another skinny, another crack like the one she fell through, where he might follow her to the place she has gone.

After one of her late episodes, the girl laid across their bed and asked, Do you ever imagine there might be a place that would be just ours? That no one else could get to?

The cartographer often imagined such places, but when he told her of his own imagined hideaways—a cabin in the mountains, or a ship floating in the middle of a vast, unknowable ocean—the girl only shook her head.

That's not what I mean, she said. I mean somewhere no one else could ever get to, no matter how hard they tried.

No one, she said, and no thing, either. Where we would be untouchable and safe.

He hadn't known what she meant then, but he did now.

What scares him even worse than not being able to find her is this: What if he finds her, only to discover that this secret place is just for her, that he can't follow where she has gone?

✚ is any hospital she went to before he met her, while ✤ stands for the hospitals and specialists she went to later, after the sleepwalking began, after the seizures got worse, after she had something to hide.

The cartographer has been to all these places. He has talked to her nurses, her doctors, her fellow patients. He has shaken the hands of these men and women and introduced himself, explained his relationship to her. Although they remember her with fond laughter and sad smiles, none of her caretakers have ever heard of him. This is how thoroughly she had protected him. This is how she kept her illness a mist-shrouded country, barely even imagined from across a vast sea.

This thing killing her the whole time they were together, it might have taken her away, but the cartographer doesn't think so.

He thinks—he believes—that there is somewhere else, some place she has escaped to. Some place where she is safe from this thing that chased her, that invaded her body, that turned her own cells against her.

He believes it took hundreds of sleepwalks for her to find this place, but that she did find it: Her skinny, the place where everything got thin enough that she could walk right through, where whatever was hurting her couldn't follow.

It has been years, but in his heart, he is still true to her. He has doubts, but he does not allow himself to express them. To do so would be the end of him, of all that he has become, of all that he has reduced himself to.

He is only the cartographer now, and so he must continue to believe.

The cartographer once thought this would be the last map he would ever create, that his profession would end with the culmination of this quest, but he knows that it might not. What awaits on the other side of the skinny might be another world, unmapped and unknown. He imagines it as a limbo, a purgatory, a place neither as bad as this world nor as good as the one they are truly destined for. It will take another map to escape that place, to complete the destiny he feels in his bones, in his sextant, in his many compasses. In their many needles, each aching to point the way.

✗:
✗ is the store where he bought the ring he never got to give her.
✗ is the place where he planned to propose, where he had already made the reservation.
✗ is the speech he rehearsed, that he practiced saying slowly, carefully, so that she would not mishear even a single syllable.
✗ is nowhere, ✗ is now, ✗ is never mind.
✗ is everything that ever mattered.
✗ is all he has left.

What follows the realization of his mistake is as intuitive as breathing, as involuntary as sleepwalking. He spreads his map before him, messy with a thousand corrections, and then, eraser in hand, he tries, tries again. One by one, he eliminates all his symbols, destroys them and replaces them with words. Mere words, great words, words that denote and words that describe and words that will direct him in the way he needs to go. Ground truth disappears, is replaced by something else, by truth as meaning, as yellow brick road, as key to a lock to a door to an entrance. He widens the error in his map one phrase at a time, each annotation requiring its own accommodations. He writes their truth upon the city, and the city bends to it, its streets and avenues warping around his words: This is the place where we met. This is the place where we kissed. This is the place where we fell in love, and so is this one and this one and this one. This is our first apartment. This is where we bought our first bed, the first thing we owned together. This is where we went for breakfast on Sunday mornings. This is our favorite restaurant, our favorite coffee shop, our favorite movie theatre. These are all the places I found you when you were lost. This is the storefront where you bought the red scarf you cherished so much, that you were wearing the day you disappeared. Where you shopped while I stood outside smoking, where I looked through the window glass and saw how beautiful you were. Where I decided I would marry you, that I would be your man forever.

This is where I was going to tell you what I wanted to tell you, where I was going to ask you the question I wanted to ask.

He annotates until the city appears as a bloated, twisted thing, depicted by a map too full of language and memory to be useful to anyone but himself. Until there are spaces that simply do not exist scattered everywhere, one of which will be the right one. After he finishes, he upends his bag on the floor of his apartment. He rifles through the spilled pile of his tools until he finds his favorite compass, the one she bought him for Christmas their first year. He holds it up, sees true north for the last time. He slips it into his pocket beside the only other thing he needs, the small black box. He puts on his coat, then steps out the door with his map in hand. He looks like a tourist, but he's not. Somewhere the city opens, like a fissure or a flower, and inside, she is waiting.

THE RECEIVING TOWER

Most nights, we climb to the tower's roof to stand together beneath the satellite dishes, where we watch the hundreds of meteorites fall through the aurora and across the arctic sky. Trapped high in the atmosphere, they streak the horizon then flare out, with only the rarest among them surviving long enough to burst into either mountains or tundra, that madness of snow and ice beneath us.

Once, Cormack stood beside me and prayed aloud that one might crash into the receiving tower instead and free us all.

Once, I knew which one of us Cormack actually was.

II

The tower is twenty stories tall, made of blast-resistant concrete and crowned by two satellite dishes twisting and turning upon their bases, their movements driven by the powerful electric motors installed between the listening room and the roof. The larger dish is used for receiving signals and messages from both our commanders and our enemies, the latter of which we are expected to decode, interpret, and then re-encrypt before sending them to our superiors using the smaller transmitting dish.

It has been months since the larger dish picked up anything but static, maybe longer. Some of the men talk openly about leaving the tower, about trying to make our way to the coast, where we might be rescued from this place by the supply transport that supposedly awaits us there. These men say the war is over, that—after all these years—we can finally go home.

The captain lets the men speak, and then, calmly, asks each of the dissenters where they are from, knowing these men will not be able to remember their hometowns, that they haven't been able to for years.

The captain, he always knows just how to quiet us.

III

As I remember it—which is not well—young Kerr was the first to grow dim. We'd find him high in the tower's listening room, cursing at the computers, locking up console after console by failing to enter his password correctly. At night, he wandered the barracks, holding a framed portrait of his son and daughter, asking us if we knew their names, if we remembered how old they were. This is when one of us would remove the photograph from its frame so that he could read the fading scrawl on the back, the inked lines he eventually wore off by tracing them over and over with his fingers, after which there was no proof to quiet his queries.

Later, after he had gotten much worse, we discovered him sleeping on the roof, half-frozen beneath the receiving dish, his arms wrapped partway around its thick stem, his mind faded, his body lean and starved and blackened with frostbite.

None of us realized he was missing until we found his body trapped in the ice just inside the compound's gate. What pain he must have felt after he threw himself from atop the tower, after he tried to crawl forward on crushed bones, heading in the direction of a coast he must have known he would never live to see.

IV

My name is Maon, according to the stitching across the breast of the uniform I am wearing and of all the others hanging in the locker beside my bunk. This is what it says beside my computer console in the listening room, and what the others call out when they greet me. It is what the captain snarls often in my direction, growling and waving his machine pistol to remind me that he is the one giving the orders, not me.

My name is Maon: Some mornings, I stand before my mirror and speak this word again and again, reminding myself as I stare at my reflection, surprised anew by the gray of my hair, by how the winter of my beard mimics the snow and ice outside. I have begun to put on fat, to find my stomach and face thicker than I believe them to be away from the mirror. Caught between the endless dark outside the tower and the constant fluorescence of our own gray halls, it is too easy to mistake one time for another, to miss meals or repeat them. My mouth tastes perpetually of cigarettes and salted beef, and my belly grows hard and pressing against the strained buttons of my uniform. Sometimes, I can't remember having ever eaten, though my stomach is so full of food I am often sick for hours.

V

It was only after Kerr died that I discovered our personnel records had been deleted: Birthdates, hometowns, the persons to be notified in the case of our deaths, all these crucial facts gone. From that moment on, we had only our tattered uniforms to prove our ranks, only the name tape attached to our chests to remind us who we each were.

Without the personnel records, it became impossible to determine the date we were to be released from service and taken to the coast for transport home. According to the captain, this meant no one could go home until we re-established contact with the main force, something he seemed increasingly uninterested in trying to do.

Once, Macrath and the others came to me and asked me to speak to the captain, to inquire after our missing records. The next morning in the mess hall, I did my best to convince him to honor their requests.

It would only take a few minutes, I said. You could do it right now. Probably there's no one out there listening, but even if there is, they won't respond without your authorization codes.

The captain finished chewing before looking up from his breakfast of runny scrambled eggs and muddy coffee. His eyes flicked from my face to where Macrath stood behind me, then back again. He said, Are you trying to give me an order, Maon?

No, sir. A suggestion, maybe.

The captain's voice was stern, providing no room for argument. When I turned to leave, I saw Macrath still standing there, his eyes murderously red-rimmed and locked onto the captain's own implacable black orbs, on those irises as shiny and flat as the surface of burnt wood. Macrath only wanted to go home. He had a family, a wife and children, a little house, a car he liked to tinker with on weekends. That was what he always told us, what he believed he remembered.

When the captain acted, it was not me he targeted but Macrath, ordering some of the men to haul him into the frozen courtyard, then following behind to deliver the fatal bullet himself. The captain explained that the orders to execute Macrath had come from higher up the chain of command, in a coded communication meant for his eyes only. Even though it was I who had manned the silence of the listening room all morning, I said nothing, counseled the others to do the same. As I had once warned Macrath: We must not cross the captain too often, and certainly not when he is in a killing mood.

VI

The captain is unshakable in the face of our questions, but perhaps he too knows nothing more than what we know ourselves: that there are no more signals, no signs of either friend or foe. When we ask if our transport is still moored at the coast, waiting for our return, he refuses to answer. He says that information is classified, and that we don't need to know. We disagree. If the ship is still waiting, then we could make a try for the coast, leaving this wasteland behind. Perhaps then we could find a way to stop our fleeing memories, to slow the dimness that replaces them. In the meantime, we blame our forgetfulness on anything we can, scapegoating the tower first and the components of our lives here second. It could be the radiation from the satellite dishes, or the constant darkness, or the fact that the only foods we eat are yeastless wafers of bread, jugs full of liquid egg substitute, tins of dried beef, plus powdered milk and powdered fruit and powdered everything else. Together, we all eat the same three meals, day after day after day, our taste buds grown as dull and listless as the brains they're connected to, until the repetition steals away our past lives, until our minds are as identical as our gray beards, our curved paunches, our time-distressed uniforms.

VII

Standing in the dark among the mechanical workings of the two satellite dishes, I work swiftly to repair a series of frayed wires splayed out from the larger dish, my fingers shaking beneath the tight beam of my headlamp, frozen even through the thickness of my gloves. It has been dark as long as I can remember, long enough that the sun grows increasingly theoretical, abstract. My own memories of it faded long ago, so that all remembrances of places lit not by torches and floodlights are suspect, at best more evidence of a past increasingly faked and unlikely, stolen from the remnants of the others who share this tower.

When I finish my task, I stand and look out from the tower's edge, studying the ice and snow and wind and, above it all, the aurora, its bright curtains of color cutting a ribbon through the darkness, obscuring much of the meteor shower that continues to fall. I linger until the cold penetrates the last of my bones, then I turn the metal wheel atop the frost-stuck hatch, descend the rickety ladder leading back into the tower.

An hour later, lying in bed, I am unable to remember the colors of the aurora, or even what exactly I went outside to fix. The events of my life increasingly exist only in the moment, too often consumed by their own bright fire, lost as the many meteorites tumbling and burning out across the already unimaginable midnight sky.

VIII

Once a week, after we're sure the captain is asleep in his quarters, we gather in the basement of the tower, amidst the stacked palettes of canned and powdered foodstuffs, the whole rooms of spare wiring kits and computer parts and drums of fuel oil, where there is enough of everything to last another hundred years. There are six of us who meet, the only ones who still remember enough to work, who can still log into our computers. Weeks ago, we changed our passwords to *password*, the first thing everyone guesses, so that as we continue to dim we will still be able to log in and listen for the orders we hope we might yet receive.

In the basement, we take turns telling whatever stories we can. Tonight, Camran tells us about playing baseball in high school, about how the smell of the grass stuck to everything, to his clothes and hair and fingers, and then about the sound of the bat striking the ball, how he once hit three home runs in a single game. With his gravelly voice, Lachlann brags about all the sex he got before coming here, going on and on about the tits and ass until we beg him to stop torturing us with what we cannot have.

Earc speaks of his parents at length, a strange but touching attachment for a man his age, and then Ros tells us about his favorite dance club back home, about the heaving crush of the dancers. We look around at the meagerness of our group, and when we try to imagine hundreds of people in one place, we find that we cannot.

I talk—as I always do—about the ship and the base camp and the coast. I have forgotten everything so that I might remember this, for myself and for the rest of us. Better that I never again recall my family, my friends, my former home, if it means remembering the ship, our last hope, because if I forget, the captain will have won and none of us will escape this tower.

We go on speaking until we've exhausted ourselves, until we've shared everything we still have left to share. Every week, this takes less and less time. Once there were eleven of us, but soon there will be only five, then four, and then three and two and one, until the treason of these meetings ceases to exist altogether.

IX

Camran is dead by the captain's hand, shot at his station in the listening room. The force of the bullet shatters his face, spraying his monitor and lodging wet flecks of skull and teeth between the once cream-colored letters of his keyboard. The captain surveys our shocked expressions, then accuses Camran of trying to use the transmitting dish to send an unauthorized message, an act of disobedience as punishable as any other. As we watch, unable to see around the bulk of his body, the captain silently reads the sentences typed across the flickering green screen, his lips moving wordlessly as his eyes scan from left to right. When he is finished, he fires a bullet into the computer, showering the leftovers of Camran with sparks. We beg him to tell us what the message said, so he gestures to his lieutenant, Dughall, the only other who'd seen the screen.

The captain puts away his pistol, then takes a deep breath, sucking in a lung's worth of cordite and bloodsmoke. He says, Let Dughall tell you, as he told me.

But of course Dughall has already forgotten—it has been months since he's been to one of our meetings—and so there is no one to tell us what message might have gotten out, or if there has been any response. All we want is something to hope for, and this the captain refuses us.

We could push the captain further but there is only so much we can risk. The threat of automatic fire from his machine pistol prevents us from asking too many questions, from arguing against even his harshest orders. We all have our sidearms, but he's the only one who still has bullets, having convinced us to surrender our own to his care some time ago, when our troubles first began.

After silencing our protests, the captain orders Dughall and some of the other dims to carry what is left of Camran down the stairs and out into the courtyard. The rest of the men go back to their work, but not me. I climb to the roof, where I watch the dims stack Camran atop the pile of our other dead, our frozen and forgotten friends.

X

The captain is in a foul mood today, in response to our persistent nagging about Camran, and to our continued speculation about the chances of making it to the coast if we were to try as a group. He rants at us for planning to abandon our posts without leave, then decides to make an example out of two of the long-time dim, Onchu and Ramsay, both so far gone they can barely speak. He dresses them in their furs, then hands them packs already provisioned to the point of bursting, as if the captain knew this day was coming. He pushes them both out the door, kicking at them and threatening with his pistol when they protest. He points toward the south, which I myself only know because it is the opposite of where I see the auroras over the mountains, then forces them across the courtyard, through the gate and out onto the ice. Within minutes they're out of sight from the ground, but from the roof we watch through our night scopes as they wander against the wind and blowing snow, unable already to remember which direction they've come from or where they're going.

Only a few hundred yards from the gate, Onchu sits on the ground, facing away from the tower, too far to see or hear us above the howl of the wind. We scream anyway, begging him to get up, to keep moving, to make for the coast, to save us all, only he doesn't move. He draws his limbs in, hanging his hooded head between his knees. By morning, he will be frozen to death, and then, some time after, we will forget his name.

Later, Ramsay somehow finds his way through the dark and the blowing snow back into the courtyard, where the captain shoots him dead, as he has so many others who have refused to go into the wastes, who have returned without his leave.

XI

Eventually, there is a meeting at which I wait alone until dawn before returning to the barracks. With no one to tell stories to, I walk the rows of bunks instead, watching my men slumber, their gray heads full of dim dreams. A week later, I find Lachlann dead by his own hand, hanging from the rafters in the supply closet. The captain cuts the body down himself, has it dragged outside and stacked with the others. He asks if anyone would like to say a few words in Lachlann's memory, shakes his head when we cannot.

XII

I wait until it is night again—true night, not just dark, as it always is—and then stuff my backpack with foodstuffs and bottles of water, with chemical torches and the thickest blankets I can find. I am leaving, but first I consider murdering the captain in his sleep, perhaps smothering him with one of his own battered pillows, or else choking him with my hands. I sneak easily past the sleeping, dim guards outside his quarters, then through the creaking door of his bedchamber.

Once inside, I stand beside the captain's bed and watch his creased, stubbled face until I experience an unexpected moment of doubt: If it is only he and I who still remember anything, then who will be left to lead these men after he is dead and I am gone? If one day the signal does come, who will be here to lead them out of the receiving tower and across the ice?

What I have to admit is that, in the face of my pending abandonment, perhaps even this captain is better than no captain at all.

Instead of killing him, I wake him up, and for the last time we talk. Seated across from me in his room, the captain makes me promise that I will leave the tower when we have finished, no matter what he tells me, and because this is already my intent, I agree.

Three questions, he says. No more.

I ask him if there are other receiving towers, and he says there are, but when I press him for details about who mans these towers, he refuses to give me a direct answer, offering only shrugging misdirections and half-truths that tell me nothing.

Next, I ask him if others will come to take our place after we are all dead. He looks over my provisioned pack, my donned furs, then says, No. You are the last Maon. I am the last captain. Everyone here is so old now, and all of them have finally grown dim. What we did, no one else will have to do.

The last question is even harder for him to answer, but I press him, begging for honesty, for confirmation, and finally he nods his head, his coal-black eyes saddened for the first time I can remember, but maybe, I realize, not for the first time ever.

He tells me how, long ago, when we were both young and strong, we stood atop the receiving tower in the dark, watching the waves of debris tear endlessly through the atmosphere, their terrible truth still disguised as innocent meteorites.

Already this was years after the war ended, after we'd each accepted we'd never go home, that there was no home to go to.

Already this was after we'd started to forget, to go dim. Not all at once, not everyone, but enough of us, starting with Kerr.

The dim demanded to know why they were being kept in the receiving tower, why they couldn't travel to the shore to be relieved of their duties. They grew restless and angry, and before long there were enough of them that something had to be done.

The captain says, Everything we did next was your decision.

He says, Before there was Maon, there was the major, and for a second I see us atop the tower, grimly shaking hands. I hear myself say to him the name that was once his, the one I have claimed myself for so long, ever since I stepped down from this command.

By my orders, he tells me, the captain took over my abandoned duties administrating the useless routines of the receiving tower, while I joined the men in the ranks so that I could better watch over the dim and keep them safe. A major no more, I held midnight meetings with those whose wits remained, explaining how, to protect our ailing friends, our brothers in arms, we would pretend the war was still being fought. To give them purpose, we would start manning the listening room again, searching for signals that did not—could not—exist, since there was no one left alive to send them.

According to the captain, this is how we saved our men, how we kept them safe long enough for our beards to gray, for our bodies to grow stooped and fat.

Still, the dim turned increasingly dangerous, first to themselves and then to the rest of us.

We waited until they began threatening murder and mutiny, then the captain had them shot and stacked one by one in the courtyard, or else pushed them out across the ice to seek the meaningless shore, the phantom promise of the waiting transport ship, a ship that existed only in the stories I told the men. That existed only to give them purpose, to give them hope they might yet be saved.

The captain says, At first, you chose who would stay and who I would force from the tower. You were still the major, even if no one remembered. You said it was my duty to give them someone to hate, if that was what it took to hold them together, to unite them in this new life they had no choice but to live.

Later, after you dimmed too, I had to decide myself when it was time to use the pistol, or to drive a man out of the tower and onto the ice.

I have done my best, he tells me, but I am not you.

I have had to be cruel.

I have had to become a monster.

All these decisions, I have had to make alone.

The captain stops speaking, turns his face toward the wall. There is only the sound of his breathing, of mine in turn, until he says, I wish you could remember for yourself.

He says, It's not as if this is the only time I've told you.

XIII

Now it is my turn to look away, ashamed, for him and for myself. For what we did together.

I say, You have done your duty well, my captain.

And you yours, he says. Better than you hoped, even.

But why switch places? How did we know? That you would remember, and I wouldn't?

He shakes his head. You've had your three questions, and now you must go.

No, I say. Tell me. How did we know?

We didn't, he says. We guessed.

The captain says nothing more. Eventually, he falls asleep in his chair, resuming his quiet snoring, his hands folded over the ampleness of his belly. I try to stay awake, to hold on to what he has told me, to try to see how these newly remembered truths might save our men, but they cannot, or perhaps they already have. Exhausted, I doze myself, and when I wake I can recall only a little of what was said between us. Maybe it is for the best. Maybe whatever he remembered is an illusion, another hallucinated landscape we dreamed up together to replace all we have lost. Perhaps all there has ever been is this receiving tower and the others like it, separated by ice and snow and mountains, and then, somewhere else, some lost continent, shapeless in my mind, where some interminable war cost us everything.

XIV

I leave the captain alive not because I have promised to, but because I am afraid that at the end of my journey, it will be proven that he has always been right, that there is no ship waiting, that to lead these men out across the tundra would be to lead them to their deaths. I walk the halls of the receiving tower one more time, making one last effort to remember, to hold onto what is left of the captain's words. I meet some of the dim going about their duties, each of them following my commands to leave me alone, obeying me as they would the captain. I take my time, knowing they will not remember seeing me, will not report my small betrayal. Eventually, I find myself wandering the rows of empty bunks at the far end of the barracks, too many beds for the number of men I can remember being lost. I try to remember who these others were, but I cannot. Their bunks are covered in dust, their bedding stripped to replace our own threadbare blankets and pillows. These bunks must belong to the dead stacked in the courtyard, but perhaps also to others like me, men who took it upon themselves to reach the sea long ago, farther back than I can remember.

There must have been so many men here, and now they are nearly all dead and forgotten by us, the very men they'd meant to rescue.

As a final act of defiance, I climb the tower to the listening room, where I make one last attempt to hear something, anything. I put on my headphones and slowly move the dials through the full spectrum of frequencies. I hear nothing but the hum and hiss of the omnipresent static, a blizzard of meaningless sound falling unceasingly upon my ears.

There was a time when I knew over one hundred words for static, but now there is only the one, so insufficient to the complexity of the thing it describes.

I take off my headphones, then move to shut down my console. Before I do, I change the password to some new word, some gibberish, something I would never have been able to remember, even in the prime of my life, all those long decades ago.

XV

I do not look back as I cross the threshold of the receiving tower, nor when I open the gate at the far end of the courtyard, but I can feel the captain watching me from atop the parapets. I wonder if he has kept vigil for all the others who began this desperate exodus, the lost men who once slept in those long empty bunks. I wonder if, like now, he kept quiet, hurling neither threats nor warnings against the piercing wind, leaving those brave men to question and to doubt, to wonder if it truly was the captain who was wrong, or only themselves.

I wonder how long he waits for me before going back inside, at what point I will no longer be able to sense his heavy eyes darkening my every step. And then I know.

XVI

I discover Onchu—who I had forgotten, who I beg forgiveness of now that he is found again—while the aurora shimmers overhead on the first night of my journey. I scrape at the snow and ice around his face, revealing the black frostbitten skin which will never decay, this place too cold and removed from the earth even for maggots or worms. After I have stared as long as I dare, I use my pick to dig his body from the ice, so that I can get at the backpack clenched in his arms, the limbs immobile with frost. I have no choice but to snap the bones with my pick, then peel them away from the bag's canvas.

I open the pack's drawstrings and plunge my hands inside, where I find fistfuls of photographs, frozen into unidentifiable clumps, then bundles of wrecked letters, misshapen ice balls of trinkets. At the bottom of the pack is a threadbare dress uniform, rolled tightly and creased with frost, unmarked except for its insignia of a major's rank, belonging to some higher-ranking officer I can no longer remember. All these artifacts might once have told me who I was, who we all were, but not now. If I reach the coast, I will have to become some new Maon, a man who remembers nothing, who did not see his only friends frozen to the earth, who did not see his compatriots gunned down by their captain, the man who—as I remember it—once swore to keep them all safe.

I leave these relics behind, scattered around Onchu's frigid form. Let our memories keep him company, if indeed they can.

XVII

Even with all the blood, it is easy to forget the sudden shift of the ice, the fall into the crevasse that followed. To forget the snapping of bones, sounding so much like the cracking of the centuries-old ice beneath my feet. Eventually, I reach down to find again the ruin of my shattered shin, and then scream until I black out, unable to remember enough to keep from shocking myself all over again once I wake.

In my few lucid moments, I stare up through the cracked ice, out of this cave and into the air beyond. I want to survive until the aurora blooms one last time, until the falling ruins of space streak across the sky again, but I have no way of telling which direction I'm facing, which slivered shard of sky I might be able to see.

Rather than risk dying in the wrong place, I decide that I might be able to splint the bone with the frame of my backpack, if I am brave and if I hurry.

I can at least hurry.

Twisting painfully, I open my pack to find all the chemical torches broken open and mixed together, so that all my meager possessions glow a ghastly shade of yellow, barely enough to work by. I cry out more than once, but eventually I manage to set the bone, binding it with the wrenched steel of my pack frame and torn strips of blanket. After that, there is only the climb, only the hard chill of ice cutting through my belly and thighs as I drag myself up the frozen incline, each inch a mile's worth of struggle, all to return to a surface as inhospitable as the underworld I am leaving.

XVIII

Back atop the ice, night falls, replacing the day's darkness with something worse. Away from the illumination of the receiving tower, night is an even blacker shade of dark, and I crave a new word for it, crave a vocabulary I have mostly forgotten, words that could have described more than simplest night, snow, ice, failure, all of which have more than one degree. I have to keep walking, one crooked step at a time, or

I will freeze. Everything I have left encircles me: my death, the aurora, and there, just beyond it, the veil which obscures this life from the next.

XIX

When I cannot will myself to try again to stand, I struggle instead from my back to a seated position and retrieve my pistol from its holster. It glows yellow where I've touched it, smeared with some chemical I no longer recognize. I pull back the slide, then put the muzzle to the fleshy muscle beneath my jaw. There is a tenderness there already, and although I wonder where it came from, I push hard anyway, feel the pain ignite my frozen nerves. I close my eyes, take a breath, and squeeze the trigger, howling as loud as the wind when the pistol produces only a dry, useless click.

I return my pistol to its holster, force myself to my feet. I start walking, leaning heavily on my one good leg, dragging the other behind, until a stumbling collapse delivers me to the ice. I struggle to sit, surrounded by the loud creak of my frozen muscles, of tendons contracting away from bone.

Then the pistol, then the confusion of the muzzle-press bruise, then the frustration of the empty chamber. Then the struggle to my feet, the few awkward steps, the next painful crash to this ice.

I drop the pistol, fail to find it in the blowing powder.

I try to draw the pistol, only to find it missing, lost somewhere behind me.

Lying on the ice in the darkness, I hear a bird cry far above me, riding the currents of rising, warmer air that must flow even here. I cannot recognize its speech, cannot remember how to differentiate between the ravens and owls who hunt the tundra and the gulls and terns found only near the shore. As useful as that information might be, I know it doesn't matter. I do not open my eyes to look, or even strain to hear the bird again. I am sure I have dreamed it, as I am dreaming all the other, older things I see flashing behind the closed curtains of my eyelids. And then the rest of me breaks free, flies away, rises above, taking the words that tied these dreams to me, and afterward there are no ships, no shores, no signals, no static, then no towers, no captains. Then there is no Maon, and then I run out of words, and then I

HIS LAST GREAT GIFT

Spear has already been living in the cabin overlooking High Rock for two weeks when the Electricizers speak of the New Motor for the first time. Awakened by their voices, Spear feels his way down the hallway from the dark and still unfamiliar bedroom to his small office. He lights a lamp and sits down at the desk. Scanning the press of ghastly faces around him, he sees they are all here tonight: Jefferson and Rush and Franklin, plus his own namesake, John Murray. They wait impatiently for him to prepare his papers, to dip a pen in ink and shake it free of the excess. When he is ready, they begin speaking, stopping occasionally to listen to other spirits that Spear cannot quite see, that he does not yet have the skills to hear. These hidden spirits are far more ancient, and Spear intuits that they guide the Electricizers in the same way that the Electricizers guide him.

What the Electricizers show Spear how to draw, they call it the New Motor, a machine unlike anything he has ever seen before. He concentrates on every word, every detail of their revealment: How this cog fits against that one, how this wire fits into this channel. In cramped, precise letters, he details which pieces should be copper, which zinc or wood or iron. The machine detailed in this first diagram is a mere miniature, no bigger than a pocket watch but twice as intricate.

It's too small, Spear says. He puts down the pen, picks up the crude blueprint with his ink-stained fingers. He holds it up to the specters. He says, How can this possibly be the messiah you promised?

Jefferson shakes his head, turns to the others. He says, It was a mistake to give this to him. Already he doubts.

Franklin and Rush mutter assent, but Murray comes to Spear's defense. Give him time, the spirit says. At first, we had doubts too.

Murray touches Spear on the face, leaving a streak of frost where his fingers graze the reverend's stubbled skin. He says, Have faith. It is big enough.

He says, Even Christ was the size of a pea once.

| THE FIRST REVEALMENT |

First, that there is a UNIVERSAL ELECTRICITY.

Second, that this electricity has never been naturally incorporated into minerals or other forms of matter.

Third, that the HUMAN ORGANISM is the most superior, natural, efficient type of mechanism known on the earth.

Fourth, that all merely scientific developments of electricity as a MOTIVE POWER are superficial, and therefore useless or impracticable.

Fifth, that the construction of a mechanism built on the laws of man's material physiology, and fed by ATMOSPHERIC ELECTRICITY, obtained by absorption and condensation, and not by friction or galvanic action, will constitute a new revelation of scientific and spiritual truths, because the plan is dissimilar to every previous human use of electricity.

This mechanism is to be called the NEW MOTOR, and it is wholly original, a mechanism the likes of which has never before existed on the earth, or in the waters under the earth, or in the air above it.

In the morning, Spear descends the hill into the village below, the several pages of diagrams rolled tight in the crook of his arm. On the way to the meeting hall, he waves hello to friends, to members of his congregation, to strangers he hopes will come and hear him speak sooner or later. He is confident, full of the revealed glory, yet when he reaches the meeting hall, he does not go in.

Spear's friends and advisors—the fellow reverends and spiritualist newspapermen meeting inside the hall—they have followed him to Massachusetts because of the revelation he claimed awaited them here. Already he knows they will not be disappointed, but he worries it is too soon to tell them about the blueprints, to allow them to doubt what the Electricizers have given him. He leaves the meeting hall without entering, wanders the town's narrow streets instead, waiting to be told what to do next.

It takes all morning, but eventually Rush appears to tell him which men to pick, which men to trust with the knowledge of what will be built in the tiny shed beside the cabin atop the hill.

He chooses two Russian immigrants, Tsesler and Voichenko, who speak no English but understand it well enough. Devoted followers of spiritualism, he has seen their big bearded heads nodding in the back row at fellowship meetings, and he knows they will be able to follow the instructions he has to give them.

After the Russians, he selects a handsome teenager named Randall, known to be hard-working and good with his hands, and James the metalworker, a man who has followed Spear since the split with the Church.

He chooses two immigrants, an orphan, and a widower: men in need of a living wage, capable of doing the work and, most importantly, with no one close enough to obligate them to share the secrets he plans to show them.

Spear selects no women on the first day, but knows he will soon. One of the women in his congregation will become his New Mary, and into her will be put this revealed god.

| THE FOURTH REVEALMENT |

Each WIRE is precious, as sacred as a spiritual verse. Each PLATE of ZINC and COPPER is clothed with symbolized meaning, so that the NEW MOTOR might correspond throughout with the principles and parts involved in the living human organism, in the joining of the MALE and FEMALE. Both the woodwork and the metallic must be extremely accurate and crafted correctly at every level from the very beginning, as any error will destroy the chance for its fruition. Only then shall it become a MATHEMATICALLY ACCURATE BODY, a MESSIAH made of singular, scientific precision instead of biological iterations and guesswork.

Before they begin, Spear gathers his chosen men together around the table in the shed, lays out the scant revealments he's received so far. He says, This is holy work, and we must endeavor at every step to do exactly what is asked of us, to ensure that we do not waste this one opportunity we are given, because it will not come again in our lifetimes.

He says, When God created the world, did he try over and over again until he got it right? Are there castaway worlds littering the cosmos, retarded with fire and ice and failed life thrashing away in the clay?

No, there are not.

When God came to save this world, did he impregnate all of Galilee, hoping that one of those seeds would grow up to be a Messiah?

No. What God needs, God makes, and it only takes the once.

Come closer. Look at what I have drawn. This is what the Electricizers have shown me.

They have revealed to us what He needs, and we must not fail in its construction.

As soon as the work begins, Spear sees the Russians have the talent necessary for the craft at hand. They work together to translate the blueprints into their own language before beginning construction, their brusque natures disguising an admirable attention to detail. At the other end of the shed, James shows Randall how to transform sheets of copper into tiny tubes and wires, teaching him as a master teaches an apprentice.

Spear looks at the tubes the two have produced so far, and he shakes his head. Smaller, he says.

Smaller is impossible, says James.

Have faith, says Spear, and faith will make it so.

James shakes his head, but with Randall's help he creates what Spear has asked for. It takes mere days to build this first machine, and when they are finished, Spear throws everyone out of the shed and padlocks the door. He does not start the machine, nor does he know how to.

He cannot, no matter how hard he tries, even see what it might do.

He thinks, Perhaps this is only the beginning, and he is right. The Electricizers return after midnight, and by morning he's ready to resume work. He calls back Tsesler and Voichenko and Randall and James and shows them the next blueprint. The new machine will be the size of a grapefruit, and the first will be its heart.

Franklin stands beside Spear on the hill, while in the shed behind them the work continues. Spear has the next two stages detailed on paper, locked in the box beneath his desk, and he is no longer concerned about their specifics. Instead, he asks Franklin about this other person, the opposite of himself. He asks Franklin, Who is the New Mary? How am I supposed to know who she will be?

Franklin waves his hand over the whole of High Rock, says, She has already been delivered unto us. You need only to claim her, to take her into your protection.

He says, When the time is right, you will know who to choose.

But the time is now, Spear says. If her pregnancy is to coincide with the creation of the motor, it must start soon.

Franklin nods. Then you must choose, and choose wisely.

* * *

On the Sabbath, Franklin stands beside Spear at the pulpit, whispering into Spear's ears, sending his words out Spear's mouth. There are tears in Spear's eyes, brought on by the great hope the Electricizers have given him. The reborn America the New Motor will bring, it is the most beautiful thing Spear has ever imagined. The abolition of slavery, the suffrage of women and negros, the institution of free love and free sex and free everything, the destruction of capitalism, of war and greed. Spear tells his congregation that, with their support, the New Motor will make all these advancements possible.

Franklin whispers something else, something meant for Spear alone. The medium nods, looks out at the congregation. One of these women must be the New Mary, and so Spear waits for Franklin to say a name, hesitating too long when the specter fails to reveal the correct choice. He considers the women in the audience, searches his heart for their qualifications. He thinks of the first Mary, of what he understands as her beauty, her innocence, her virginity. The girl he selects to replace her must be young, and she must be unmarried.

Spear does not know the women of his congregation well.

He can recognize them by sight, but remembers their names only when he sees them beside their husbands or fathers or brothers.

There is only one he has known for a long time, one he has watched grow from a child into a young woman, all under the tutelage of the spiritualist movement. He has always felt discomfited by the attention he paid her, but at last he sees the reasons for his lingering gazes, his wanting thoughts. From the pulpit, he says her name: Abigail Dermot.

He says, Abigail Dermot, please step forward.

He doesn't watch her stand, confused, doesn't watch her walk up the aisle. He averts his eyes, both from her and from the front pew, where his wife and children sit.

The thoughts in his head, he does not want to share them with his wife.

He turns to Franklin, but the specter is gone. What he does next, he does on his own.

| THE SEVENTEETH REVEALMENT |

Among you there will be a NEW MARY, one who has inherited at the outset an unusually sensitive nature, refined by suffering. To her will be revealed the true meaning of the CROSS, as the intersection of heaven and earth, as positive and negative, as both male and female. She will become a MOTHER, but in a new sense: the MARY OF A NEW DISPENSATION. She will feel a maternal feeling toward not just the NEW MOTOR but also to all individuals, who, through her instrumentality, will one day be instructed in the truth of the new philosophy.

After the services are over, Spear takes Abigail into his office in the meetinghouse and motions for her to sit down before taking his own seat behind the desk. He believes she is sixteen or seventeen, but when he asks, she says, Fifteen, Reverend. She has not looked at him once since he called her up to the front of the congregation, since he told the others that she was the chosen one who would give birth to the revelation they all awaited.

Spear says, Abigail, you are marked, by God and by his agents and by me. You are special, set apart from the others.

He says, Abigail. Look at me.

She raises her eyes, and he can see how scared she is of what she's been called to do. He stands and walks around the desk to kneel before her. She smells of lavender, jasmine, the first dust off a fresh blossom. His hands clasped in front of himself, he says, Can you accept what's being offered to you?

He rises, touches her shoulder, then lifts her chin so that their faces are aligned, so that her blonde hair falls away from her eyes.

He says, It is God that calls you, not me, and it is him you must answer.

But Spear wonders. It is only he and her, alone, and without the Electricizers he can only trust what he himself feels in the hollows of his own imperfect heart.

| THE THIRTY-SECOND REVEALMENT |

The MEDIUM is rough, coarse, lacking culture and hospitality, but with the elements deemed essential for the engineering of the NEW MOTOR, for this important branch of labor. At times he must be in the objective position [not in a TRANCE] while at other times he must be erratic, must ignore his family and friends so that he might hear our many voices. Acting upon impulse, this person will be made to say and do things of an extraordinary character. He will not be held accountable for his actions during the MONTHS OF CREATION. Treading on ground so delicate, he cannot be expected to comprehend the purposes aimed at. Do not hold him as a sinner during this time, for all will be forgiven, every secret action necessarily enjoined.

The services of many persons must be secured to the carrying forth of a work so novel, so important. The NEW MOTOR will be the BEACON-FIRE, the BLOOD-RED CROSS, the GENERAL ORDER OF THE NEW DAY. Whatever must be sacrificed must be sacrificed, whatever must be cast aside must be cast aside. Trust the MEDIUM, for through him we speak great speech.

That night, Rush shows Spear the next stages of the New Motor, detailing the flywheel that will have to be cast at great cost. Spear is given ideas, designs, structures, scientific laws and principles, all of which he writes as quickly as he can, his hand moving faster than his mind can follow. When he reads over what he has written, he recognizes that the blueprint is something that could not have originated from within him. He can barely comprehend it as it is now, fully formed upon the paper, much less conceive how he would have arrived at this grand design without the help of the Electricizers.

Rush says, The motor will cause great floods of spiritual light to descend from the heavens. It will reveal the earth to be a limitless trove of motion, life, and freedom.

Spear dutifully inks the diagram and annotates each of its intricacies, then asks, Did I choose the right girl?

Rush points to the diagram and says, That should be copper, not zinc.

Spear makes the correction, then presses his issue. She's only fifteen, from a good family. Surely she's a virgin.

He says, I have seen her pray, and I believe she is as pure of heart as any in the congregation.

Rush says, We want to reveal more, but only if you can concentrate. It isn't easy for us to be here. Don't waste our time.

Spear apologizes, swallows his doubts. He silences his heart and opens his ears. He writes what he needs to write, draws what he needs to draw.

A week later, Spear sends Randall down into the village to fetch Abigail. When the boy returns with the girl, her mother and father also walk beside her. Spear tries to ignore the parents as he takes the girl by the arm, but her father steps around him, blocking the path to the shed.

The father says, Reverend, if God needs my daughter, then so be it. But I want to see where you're taking her.

Spear shakes his head, keeps his hand on the girl. Says, Mr. Dermot, I assure you that your daughter is safe with me. We go with God.

What is in there that a child needs to see but a man cannot?

You will see it, Mr. Dermot. Everyone will, when the time comes. When my task—your daughter's task—is complete, then you will see it. But not before.

Spear holds the father's gaze for a long time. He wants to look at Abigail, to assure her that there is nothing to be afraid of, but he knows it is the father he must convince. Behind them, her mother is crying quietly, her sobs barely louder than the slight wind blowing across the hill. Spear waits with a prayer on his lips, with a call for help reserved farther down his throat. Randall is nearby, and the Russians and the metalworker will come if he calls.

Eventually the father steps aside. Spear breaks his gaze but says nothing as he moves forward with the girl in tow. Out of the corner of his eye, he sees the curtain of his cabin parted, sees his wife's face obscured by the cheap glass of the window. He does not look more closely, does not acknowledge the expression he knows is there.

Inside the work shed, construction continues as Spear shows Abigail what has been done, what the New Motor is becoming. He explains her role as the New Mary, that she has been chosen to give life to the machine.

He says, I am the architect, but I am no more the father than Joseph was. This is your child, and God's child.

He says, Do you understand what I am telling you?

The Electricizers are gathered in the shed, watching him. He looks to them for approval, but their focus is on the machine itself. Inside the shed, the words he says to them never have any effect, never move them to response or reaction.

Work stalls while they wait for supplies to come by train to Randolph, and then overland to High Rock by wagon. For two weeks, Spear has nothing to do but return to the ordinary business of running his congregation, which includes acting as a medium for congregation members who wish to contact their deceased, or to seek advice from the spirit world. A woman crosses his palm with coin and he offers her comforting words from her passed husband, then he helps a businessman get advice from an old partner. Normally, Spear has no trouble crossing the veil and coming back with the words the spirits offer him, but something has changed with the arrival of the Electricizers, a condition aggravated since the beginning of construction on the Motor. He hears the other spirits as if his ears are filled with cotton or wax, as if there is something in the way of true communication, and the real world seems just as distant, just as difficult to navigate.

By the time the spinster Maud Trenton comes to see him, he can barely see her, can barely hear her when she says, I'm hearing voices, Reverend. Receiving visitations.

She says, Angels have come to me in the night.

Spear shakes his head, sure he has misunderstood the woman. He feels like a child trapped in a curtain, unable to jerk himself free. He hasn't crossed the veil, merely caught himself up in it.

He says, What did you say?

Maud Trenton, in her fifties, with a face pocked by acne scars and a mouth full of the mere memories of teeth, she says, I told the angels I was afraid, and the angels told me to come to see you.

Jefferson appears behind her, with his sleeves rolled up, wig set aside. His glow is so bright it is hard for Spear to look directly at the specter, who says, Tell her that God loves her.

Spear's eyes roll and blink and try to right themselves. He can feel his pupils dilating, letting more light come streaking in as wide bands of colors splay across his field of vision. He's firmly on the other side, closer to what comes next than what is.

Jefferson says, Tell her we're thankful. Tell her we venerate her and protect her and watch over her. Tell her the whole host is at her service.

Spear is so confused that when he opens his mouth to say Jefferson's words, nothing comes out. And then the specter is gone, and Spear is freed from his vision, returned to the more substantial world, where Maud sits across from him, her eyes cast downward into her lap, her hands busy worrying a handkerchief to tatters. Suddenly Spear feels tired, too tired to talk to this woman anymore, or to concern himself with her problems.

Spear opens his mouth to say Jefferson's words, but they won't come out, and although he knows why he blames her instead. He says, Woman, I have nothing to say to you. If you feel what you're doing is wrong—if you've come to me for absolution—then go home and pray for yourself, for I have not been granted it to give you.

At dinner that night, Spear's forehead throbs while his wife and daughters chatter around him, desperate for his attention after his day spent down in the village. He continues to nod and smile, hoping his reaction is appropriate to the conversation. He can't hear his family's words, cannot comprehend their facial expressions no matter how hard he tries.

He does not try that hard.

What is in the way is the New Motor. The revealments are coming faster now, and Spear understands that there are many more to come. It will take eight more months to finish the machine, an interminable time to wait, but there is so much to do that Spear is grateful for every remaining second.

The New Motor is ready to be mounted on a special table commissioned specifically for the project, and so Spear brings two carpenters into his expanding crew, each once again hand-selected from the men of High Rock. The table is sturdy oak, its thick top carved with several deep, concentric circles designed to surround the growing machine. When the carpenters ask him what the grooves mean, or what they do, Spear shakes his head. Their purpose has not been revealed, only their need.

Abigail becomes a fixture in the shed, spending every day with the men and the Motor. Spear sets aside part of every morning for her instruction, relating scriptures he finds applicable. The girl is an attentive student, listening carefully and asking insightful questions. Spear finds himself wishing his own children were so worthy, and more than once he finds the slow linger of a smile burnt across his cheeks long after he and Abigail have finished speaking.

In the afternoons, he joins the others in the day-to-day work of constructing the machine, but even then he continues to watch her, to notice her. This is how he observes the way she sees Randall, the talented young worker who will have his pick of trades when the time comes. Metalworking, carpentry, even the doing of figures and interpretation of the diagrams come easy to Randall, the boy's aptitudes speaking well of his deeper, better qualities. Spear has often been impressed with the boy, but now, watching the quick glances and quicker smiles that pass between Randall and Abigail, he knows he will have to study him even closer.

He tells himself that it is not the girl he cares about, but the Motor. After she gives birth to his machine, Randall can have her. But not before. Spear is sure that, like Mary, Abigail must be a virgin to bring the Motor to life, and he cannot risk Randall ruining that. He decides that he will take the girl home to live with him, just until summer. She will become part of his household, and he himself will keep her safe. Although he trusts all those he surrounds himself with, it is only himself that he can vouch is above reproach.

Spear is no engineer, but he knows enough to understand that the New Motor is different. Where most machines are built in pieces, one component at a time, the Motor is being built from the inside out. It is being grown, with the sweat and effort of these great Spiritualist men, all excellent workers, excellent minds. Tsesler and Voichenko especially seem given to the task; their ability to translate the complexities of the diagrams and explanations into their own language is almost uncanny. The others work nearly as hard, including Randall. Despite Spear's misgivings about the boy, he knows the young man is as dedicated as any other to the completion of their work. Six days a week, for ten or twelve or fourteen hours, they slave together in the forge-heated shed to fulfill the task handed down to them by the Electricizers. By the time snow covers the hill, the machine has enough moving parts that a once useless flywheel becomes predictive, turning cogs that foretell the other cogs and gears and pulleys not yet known to Spear. The first gliding panel is set in the innermost groove of the table's concentric circles, moved all the way around the Motor once to ensure that it works the way it is intended to. The panel's copper face is inscribed with words that Spear does not know, but which he believes are the long-hidden names of God, revealed here in glory and in grace.

On the day of the fall equinox, the men work and work. When they finish after dark, Spear gathers them all around himself. He is covered in sweat and dirt and grease and grime. They all are, and Spear smiles, prouder than he has ever allowed himself to be.

He looks over his men, and he says, It took a quarter of a million years for God to design our last messiah, and even then, he could only come in our form, created in our image, a fallen man. Our new messiah will take only nine months to build, and when it is done it will show us who our own children will be, what they will become in the new kingdom.

This New Motor, it will be the beginning of a new race, unfallen and perfect, characterized by a steamwork perfection our world is only now capable of creating. God has shown the Electricizers and they have shown me and I have shown you, and now you are making it so.

The New Motor is his task, but Spear knows that there are others working too, all of them assigned their own tasks somewhere out in America. He knows this because even on the nights when the others fail to materialize, Franklin comes and takes Spear from his bed and out into the night. The two men walk the empty streets, Spear shivering in his long wool coat and hat and boots, Franklin unaffected by the cold. The specter tells him of other groups sent to help, of other spirits in need of a medium: the Healthfulizers, the Educationalizers, the Agriculturalizers, the Elementizers, the Governmentizers, perhaps other groups unfamiliar even to Franklin.

Franklin says, I can't know everything.

Like you, he says, I am merely a vessel.

He puts a cold hand on Spear's shoulder, causing the medium's teeth to chatter together hard, too hard. If the specter doesn't release him soon, Spear worries that he'll break his molars.

A new age is coming, Franklin says. The Garden restored.

He says, Fear not.

He says, Through God, even one such as you might be made ready.

As the Motor grows in complexity, Spear begins to lose his temper more and more often, always at home, always behind closed doors. He tells his wife again and again that Abigail is not to work, that she is not to lift a finger, but more than once he comes home to find the girl helping his wife with her chores.

To his wife, he says, Why is it that you can't listen to even the simplest of my instructions?

Pointing to Abigail, he says, She's pregnant, with the growing king of our new world. Why can't you do what I say, and treat her accordingly?

His wife begins to weep, but her fury is uncooled by the tears streaming down her face. She says, sounding as tired as he's ever heard, She's not pregnant, John. The only reason she's here is that you want her instead of me.

To Abigail, Spear says, Child, return to your room.

He waits until Abigail has left the room before he strikes his wife across the face with the back of his hand, then says, Christ forgive me, but you watch your tongue. You either recognize the glory of God or you do not. Only you can choose which it will be, and in the end, you must choose.

By December, there have been sixty-five revealments, and by the end of January there are thirty more. The New Motor is growing larger, taking up the entire table with its array of sliding panels and connecting tubes and gears. Loose bundles of wires dangle from the construct's innards, waiting for the places where they will connect and give life to extremities that only Spear has seen so far, to other appendages even he can't yet imagine.

This machine, it does not resemble a man, as Spear once thought it would. What's worse, it doesn't resemble anything anyone has seen before, causing the other workers to question him. He does his best to quell their worries, but as the team grows they ask their questions louder and louder, until their concerns leak out of the shed and into the congregation below. The collections that once went to feeding the poor or funding abolitionist trips into the South have for months gone to the Motor, and so the congregation's patience grows thin, especially among those who haven't seen it, who cannot conceive of what it is, what it will be.

Spear counsels patience, counsels faith. From the pulpit, he says, We have been given a great gift, and we must not question it.

But he does. He questions, he doubts. His resolve wavers. He opens his mouth to speak again, but cannot. He hasn't eaten or changed his clothes in days, and has taken to sleeping in the shed beneath the copper reflection of the Motor. He does not go home to the cabin except to fetch Abigail in the mornings and to take her back home at night.

On the next Sabbath, he stumbles at the pulpit, but the Electricizers at his side catch him with their frosty hands and return him to his station.

Spear shivers, wipes the drool off his lip with the back of a shaky hand. He waves his hand, motions for the ushers to pass the collection plate. They hesitate, look to the deacons for confirmation, a gesture not lost on Spear, who knows his authority has been questioned, his future dependent on the successful outcome of his great project.

Spear closes his eyes against his congregation's wavering faith, then says, God blesses you, in this kingdom, and in the one to come. Give freely, for what you have here you will not soon need.

Spear has to stifle a gasp when Maud Trenton comes into his office during the first week of February. She is as pregnant as any woman Spear has ever seen, her belly stressing the seams of her black dress. He can see patches of skin between strained buttons, and momentarily he desires to reach out and touch her stomach, to feel the heat of the baby inside.

Maud sits, her hands and arms wrapped around the round bulk of her belly. She says, I need your help, Reverend.

With quivering lips, she says, I don't know where this baby came from, and I don't know what to do with it.

Spear shudders, trying to imagine who would have impregnated this woman. He realizes it has been weeks since he last saw Maud at services or group meetings. She's been hiding herself away, keeping her shame a secret. The people in the village may not be ready to accept such a thing, but Spear prides himself on his progressive politics, on the radical nature of his insight. He believes a woman should be able to make love to who she wants, that a child can be raised by a village when a father is unavailable. This does not have to be the ruin of this woman, but there must be truth, confession, an accounting.

Spear says, Do you know who the father is?

Maud neither nods nor shakes her head. She makes no motion to the affirmative or the negative. She says, There is no father.

Through the curtain of gray hair falling across her downcast face, she says, I am a virgin.

She looks up and says, I know you know this.

Spear shakes his head. He does not want to believe and so he does not. He says, If you cannot admit your sin, then how can you do penance?

He says, The church can help you, but only if you allow it to. I ask again, Who is the father?

Spear asks and asks, but she refuses to tell the truth, even when he walks around the desk and shakes her by the shoulder. She says nothing, so he sends her away. She will return when she is ready, and when she is ready he will make sure she is taken care of. There is time to save the child, if only she will listen.

At night, Spear wanders the floors of the small cabin, checking and rechecking the doors. He locks Abigail's door himself each evening but often still awakens in the night, sure her door is open wide. He rushes out into the hall only to find it locked, as he left it. These nights, he stands outside her door with his face pressed to the wood, listening to the sounds of her breathing. Sometimes, he dreams he has been inside the room, that he has said or done something improper, only later he can never remember what. More than once, he wakes up in the morning curled in front of her door, like a guard dog or else a penitent, waiting to be forgiven.

The Electricizers fill Spear's bedroom with more specters than ever before. He can see some of the others, the older spirits he long ago intuited, can hear the creaky whisper of their instructions. These are past leaders of men, undead but still burdened by their great designs, and Spear can sense the revealments these older ghosts once loosed from their spectral tongues: their Towers of Babel, their great Arks. His fingers cramp into claws as he struggles to write fast enough to keep up with the hours of instruction he receives, his pen scratching across countless pages. Near dawn, he looks down and for one moment he sees himself not as a man but as one of the Electricizers. His freezing, fading muscles ache with iced lightning, shooting jolts of pain through his joints. Spear understands that Franklin and Jefferson and Murray and the rest are merely the latest in a long line of those chosen to lead in both this life and the next, and Spear wonders if he too is being groomed to continue their great works. He looks at Franklin, whose face is only inches away from his own. He sees himself in the specter's spectacles, sees how wan and wasted he looks.

Spear says, Am I dying?

The ghost shakes his head, suddenly sadder than Spear has ever seen him. Franklin says, There is no longer such a thing as death. Now write.

February and March pass quietly, the work slowing then halting altogether as supplies take longer and longer to reach High Rock through the snow-choked woods. Spear spends the idlest days pacing alone in the snow atop the hill, watching the road from Randolph obsessively. There is so much left to do, and always less time to do it in.

In June, the nine months will be over. The Motor must be ready. God waits for no man, and Spear does not want to disappoint.

Spear spends the short winter days in the shed, checking and rechecking the construction of the Motor, but the long evenings are another matter. Being trapped in the cabin with his wife and children is unbearable, and being trapped there with Abigail is a torture of another kind. From his chair in the sitting room, he finds his eyes drawn to her flat belly, to the lack of sign or signal. From there he wanders to her covered breasts, and then to the lines of pale skin that escape the neckline of her dress, the hems at the wrists of her long sleeves. He watches her while she plays with his own children on the floor, watches for the kindness and grace he expects to find in his New Mary.

Mostly, what he sees is boredom, the same emotion that has overwhelmed him all winter, trapped by snow and waiting for the coming thaw that feels too far off to count on. While they wait, he expects some sign, something to show her development into what she must become. He knows she will not give birth to the Motor, not exactly, but she must give it life somehow.

Spear wishes he could ask the Electricizers for reassurance, but he knows they will not answer. Despite their long-winded exposition on every facet of the Motor's construction, they have been silent on the subject of Abigail since he first plucked her from the flock.

Spear decides nothing. He stops touching his wife, stops holding his children. He tells himself he is too tired, too cold. Food tastes like ash, so he stops eating. The Electricizers keep him up all night with their diagrams and their inscriptions and their persistent pushing for speed, for completion.

Jefferson tells Spear that by the end of the month he will know everything he needs to know to finish the New Motor. The revelation will be complete.

By the end of the month, Spear replies, I will be a ghost. He spits toward the ancient glimmer, sneers.

The specters ignore his doubt. They press him, and when he resists, they press harder, until eventually he goes back to work. He writes the words they speak. He draws the images they describe. He does whatever they ask, but in his worst moments he does it only because he believes that by giving in he might one day reach the moment where they will at last leave him alone.

| THE ONE HUNDRED
SEVENTY-SIXTH REVEALMENT |

The PSYCHIC BATTERY must be cylindrical in shape, constructed of lead and filled with two channels of liquid, one containing a copper sulfate and the other zinc. Copper wires will be run from the GRAND REVOLVER into each channel, with great care taken to ensure that none of the wires touch each other as they ascend into the NEW MOTOR. There is a danger of electrocution, of acid burns, of the loss of life and the destruction of the machine. From the moment of CONCEPTION to the moment of BIRTH, always the NEW MOTOR has been in danger, and in these stages there is no safety except for the careful, the diligent, the righteous. When the PSYCHIC BATTERY has been successfully installed, the NEW MOTOR will be complete in one part of its nature, as complete as the MEDIUM alone can make it. Men have done their work, and now it is the women's turn.

In the morning, the other leaders of the congregation are waiting for Spear when he steps out of the cabin. On his porch are other preachers, mediums, the newspapermen who months before published excited articles in support of the project. The men stand in a half-circle in front of his house, smoking their pipes and chatting. Their voices drop into silence as Spear descends the steps from his porch onto the lawn.

One of the preachers speaks, saying, John, this has to stop. Whatever you're doing in that shed, it's bankrupting the community.

The newspaperman nods and says, We thought this was a gift from God, that his spirit spoke through you, but—

He breaks off, looks to the others for support. He says, John, what if what you're making is an abomination instead of a revelation?

And what about the girl, John? What are you doing with the girl?

The others mutter their assent, close ranks against him. Spear doesn't move. They aren't physically threatening him, despite their new proximity. He closes his eyes, and waits a long minute before responding. He holds out his small hands, displays the creases of grease and dirt that for the first time in his life cross his palms.

Spear says, I am a person destitute of creative genius, bereft of scientific knowledge in the fields of magnetism and engineering and electricity. I cannot even accomplish the simplest of handy mechanics. Everything I tell you is true, as I do not have the predisposition to make any suggestions of my own for how this device might function or how to build what we have built.

He says, This gift I bring you, it could not have come from me, but it does come through me.

It comes through me, or not at all.

The men say nothing. They tap their pipe ash into the snow, or shuffle their feet and stare down the hill. There is no sound coming from the shed, even though Spear knows the workers have all arrived. They're listening too, waiting to hear what happens next.

Spear says, Four more months. All I need is four more months. The Motor will be alive by the end of June.

He promises, and then he waits for the men to each take his hand and agree, which they eventually do, although it costs him the rest of his credibility, what little is left of the goodwill earned through a lifetime of service. It does not matter that their grips are reluctant, that their eyes flash new warnings. Whatever doubts he might have when he is alone, they disappear when he is questioned by others, as they always have. The Electricizers will not disappoint, nor the God who directs them.

While he is shaking hands with the last of the men, he hears the cabin door open again. Thinking it is Abigail coming to join him in the shed, Spear turns around with a smile on his face, then loses it when he sees his wife instead, standing on the porch, holding his oldest child by the hand. Their other child is balanced in the crook of her arm, and all are dressed for travel. He looks from his wife to the men in his yard—his friends—and then back again. While the men help his wife with the two chests she has packed, Spear stands still and watches without a word. Even when his family stands before him, he has no words.

He blinks, blinks again, then he looks at this woman. He looks at her children. He turns, puts his back to them, waits until they are far enough that they could be anyone's family before he looks once more.

He watches until they disappear into the town, and then he goes into the shed and begins the day's work, already much delayed. He sets his valise down on the work table at the back of the shed, unpacks his papers detailing the newest revealments. While the men gather to look at the blueprints, he wanders off to stare at the Motor itself. It gleams in the windowless shed, the lamplight reflecting off the copper and zinc, off the multitudes of burnished magnetic spheres. He puts his hand to the inscriptions in the table, runs his fingers down the central shaft, what the Electricizers call the grand revolver. It towers over the table, vaguely forming the shape of a cross. There are holes punctured through the tubing, where more spheres will be hung before the outer casing is cast and installed. It is this casing that he has brought the plans for today.

Spear does not need an explanation from the Electricizers to understand this part. Even he can see that the symbols and patterns upon the panels are the emblematic form of the universe itself. They are the mind of God, the human microcosm, described at last in simple, geometric beauty. He does not explain it to these men who work for him, does not think they need to know everything that he does.

The only person he will explain it to is Abigail, and then only if she asks.

With his family gone back to Boston, the cabin is suddenly too big for Spear and Abigail, with its cavernous cold rooms, but also too small, with no one to mediate or mitigate their bodies and movements. Everywhere Spear goes, he runs into the girl, into her small, supposedly virginal form. Despite her bright inquisitiveness whenever she visits the shed, she is quieter in the cabin, continuing her deference to his status as both a male and a church leader. Abigail keeps her eyes averted and her hands clasped in front of her, preventing her from noticing that in their forced solitude Spear stares openly at her, trying to will her to look at him, to answer his hungry looks with one of her own, only to punish himself later for his inability to control these thoughts.

By March, he is actively avoiding her within his own home, so much so that he almost doesn't notice when she begins to show around the belly. The bulge is just a hand's breadth of flesh, just the start of something greater yet to come.

He is elated when he sees it, but the feeling does not last.

Spear knows he has chosen wrong, has known for months that the Electricizers' refusal to discuss the girl is his own fault. In the shed, he stops to take in the New Motor, growing ever more massive, more intricate. There is much left to do before June, and now much to pray and atone for as well. He is sorry for his own mistakes, but knows Abigail's pregnancy is another matter altogether, a sin to be punished separately from his own. Spear drags Randall out of the shed by his collar and flings him into the muddy earth. The boy is bigger than he, healthier and stronger, but Spear has the advantage of surprise and it is all he needs. He cannot stop to accuse, to question, must instead keep the boy on the ground, stomping his foot into the teenager's face and stomach and ribs. The boy cries out his innocence, but Spear keeps at it until he hears the unasked for confession spray from between the boy's teeth.

When Randall returns to the shed, Spear will welcome the boy with open arms. He will forgive the boy, and then he will send him to collect Abigail and return her to her father's home. Let Abigail's father deal with what she and Randall have done, for Spear has his own child to protect.

* * *

Even after Abigail leaves, Spear waits to go to Maud Trenton. He walks down the hill to his offices in the meeting hall, a place he hasn't been in weeks, and sends one of the deacons to summon her. When she enters his office and closes the door behind her, Spear barely recognizes the woman before him.

Her face is clear, her acne scars disappeared, and the thin gray hair that once hung down her face is now a thick, shining brown, healthy and full. Even her teeth have healed themselves, or else new ones have appeared in her mouth, grown in strong and white. She is shy, but when he catches her gaze, he sees the glory in her eyes, the power of the life that rests in her belly.

Spear says, Forgive me, Mother, for I did not know who you were.

He gets down on his knees before her and presses his head against the folds of her dress. He feels his body shudder but does not recognize the feeling, the new shape of sadness and shame that accompanies his sobs. While he cries, she reaches down and strokes his hair, her touch as soothing as his own mother's once was. In a lowly voice, he gives thanks that his lack of faith was not enough to doom their project, or to change the truth, finally revealed to him: This woman is the Mother and he is the Father and together they will bring new life to the world. He reaches down and lifts the hem of her dress, working upward, bunching the starched material in his fists. He exposes her thick legs, her thighs strong as tree stumps but smooth and clean, their smell like soap, like buttermilk and cloves. He keeps pushing her dress up until he holds the material under her enlarged breasts, until he exposes the mountain of her swollen belly, her navel popped out like a thumb. He puts his face against the hot, hard flesh, feels her warmth radiate against his skin. She moans when he opens his mouth and kisses the belly, and he feels himself growing hard, the beginning of an erection that is not sex but glory. Maud's legs quiver, buck, threaten to collapse, and he lets the fabric of her dress fall over him as he reaches around to support her. He stays for a long time with his face against her belly and his hands clenched around her thighs. He waits until she uncovers him herself, until she takes his weeping face in her hands. She lifts gently, and he follows the movement until he is once again apart from her, standing on his feet.

Maud kisses Spear on the forehead, then crosses herself before turning away, keeping her back to him until Spear leaves her there in his own office. He walks outside into the warmth of a sun he has not felt in months. He has supplicated himself, has seen the mystery with his own eyes, and he has been blessed by this woman, the one he failed to choose so long ago. It is enough to put faith in God and in what God has asked of him. It is enough to cast aside all doubts, forever more.

Jefferson wakes Spear with a touch to his shoulder, the specter's hand a dagger of ice sliding effortlessly through muscle and bone. Jefferson says, Come. I want to show you what will happen next.

The reverend gets up and follows the spirit outside, where they stand together on the hill and look down at High Rock, at the roads that lead toward Randolph and the railroad and the rest of America.

Jefferson says, As the Christ was born in Bethlehem and raised in Nazareth, so the New Motor has been built here by the people of High Rock. When it is finished, it must go forth to unite the people, and you with it.

Spear says, But how? It gets bigger every day. Surely it's too large to rest on a wagon.

Jefferson shakes his head. He says, Once the machine has been animated, you will disassemble it one more time, and then you will take it to Randolph where you will rebuild it inside a railroad car.

Spear says, The railroad doesn't go far enough. We'll never make it across the country that way.

Jefferson ignores his objection, saying, One day it will, and in the meantime the Motor will grow stronger and stronger. You will take our New Messiah from town to town, and He will reach out and speak through you to the masses. He will use your mouth and your tongue to relay His words, to bring about the new Kingdom that awaits this country. This is why your family was taken from you. This was why we could not allow you to keep the girl, even after the Motor was finished.

He says, As much as you have given, there is more that may be asked of you. You must give up everything you have to follow the Motor, as the disciples did before you.

Spear looks at Jefferson, stares at his ghostly, glowing form. He wants to say that there is nothing left to give, that already he is a shell of a man, reduced to a mere vessel, an empty reservoir, but it is too late to protest, too late to go back. Whatever else remains, he does not care enough for himself to refuse any of it.

| THE TWO HUNDREDTH REVEALMENT |

BIRTH will commence upon the arrival of the NEW MARY, who will arrive pregnant with the energy necessary to bring the machine to life. Through the WOMBOMIC PROCESSES, the NEW MARY will be filled with the THOUGHT-CHILD, the necessary intellectual, moral, social, religious, spiritual, and celestial energies that will fill the PSYCHIC BATTERY and give BIRTH to the new age. The BIRTH will be attended by the MEDIUM, who will become more-than-a-male—a FATHER—even as the NEW MARY becomes more-than-a-female—a MOTHER. The womb has had its season of desire. It has had its electrical impartation. The organism of a choice person was acted upon by our LORD and MAKER. The NEW MARY is a person of extraordinary electric power, united in a harmonious, well-balanced physical, mental, and spiritual organism, and when she is brought within the sphere of the NEW MOTOR she will give it life.

The first week of June, Maud Trenton struggles up the hill in the pre-dawn dark, her arms wrapped under the largess of her belly, supporting the baby inside. She climbs alone, as she has done everything else in her long life, but she also feels watched, as she has since even before the stirring in her body began. She feels the presence of spirits, of angels, of men who care for her, protect her, keep her safe. When she stumbles to the stony path, it is these angels who give her the strength to rise again, lifting her with hands as warm and soft as they are invisible. The rest of the climb, they hold her by the elbows as she walks, keeping her ankles from twisting, from casting her again to the ground beneath her feet.

At the top of the hill, both the cabin and the shed are dark and quiet. She looks up into the sky, into the pink dawn obliterating the star-flecked heavens by degrees. She moans, squatting over her knees to wait out the horrible pressure of the next contraction. She wants to go to the cabin to wake Reverend Spear, but even a mother as inexperienced as she knows time is short. The angels whisper to her, guide her away from the cabin and toward the shed instead. She must be inside when she gives birth, must be near this new messiah that the reverend has revealed to her.

She tries to open the shed's wide, sliding door, but can't. For a moment, she sees the lock clasped around the latch and despairs, but then—after another crushing contraction—the door slides open at her touch, helped along its tracks by her angels. Inside, the room is dark and cool, the dimness softened by the slow sunlight following her inside. At the direction of the angels, she moves to lie down on the floor, to lean her head back on the dusty floorboards, but only after she stares at the machine, at its metallic, crafted magnificence. She does not understand its purpose, but its beauty is undeniable.

There is no midwife to guide her, no husband to comfort her, but Maud does not miss them. She requires no earthly assistance. The angels are beside her, and with them is her God. It is enough. Her whole life, he has come when she has called, and it has always been enough.

* * *

Spear watches from the cabin windows, waiting for the Electricizers to leave Maud's side and fetch him, but they stay with her and envelop her with their light. Eventually, Spear leaves the cabin himself and goes to the shed, where he sits down beside Maud and takes her in his arms, holds her sweating, convulsing body to his. He watches her clenched jaws and closed eyes, watches her legs kick out from her body. He tries to remember the birth of his own children, finds he cannot, then puts his past from his mind. He whispers to Maud, telling her about the great purpose of what she is doing, about the great world she is bringing into being.

At last, he says, Push, and then she does. She spreads her legs, and her womb empties, and afterward Spear and Maud and the Electricizers all wait together, a long moment where Spear feels nothing except for the breath trapped in his lungs, the woman in his arms, the way his heart beats both fast and slow at the same time, as if it might stop at any moment, as if it might go on forever.

The New Motor begins to pulsate subtly, a motion so slight Spear can only see it if he looks at the machine sideways, out of the corner of his eyes. He smiles with a slow, crooked hesitance, nine months of doubt reassured only by this pulsation, by this slight swaying in the hanging magnets of the grand revolver. It is not much, and certainly it is less than he hoped for, but it is something.

Spear hopes—Spear prays—that this is only the beginning, that this infant energy will mature into the great savior he has been promised, that he has promised himself.

Her pregnancy ended, Maud Trenton is light, her body barely skin, barely bones, her cries producing so little water they are barely tears. He lifts her in his arms, carries her gently from the shed into the cabin, where he lays her down on the bed he once shared with his own wife. He waits with her until she falls asleep. It takes a long time, and it takes even longer for Spear to realize she was not crying in pain, but in frustration. A lifetime of waiting and a near-year of effort, and still she is without a child to call her own. Now Spear understands the terror that is the Virgin, the horror that is the name Mary, the new awfulness that he and the Electricizers have made of this woman.

Whatever this thing is she has given birth to, it will never be hers alone.

He whispers apologies, pleas for penance into her dreaming ears, and then he gets up to leave her. He will go down into the village and fetch the doctor, but only after he attends to the Motor.

First, he must lock the shed's doors and be sure that no man crosses that threshold until he is ready, until he can explain what exactly it is that has happened to his machine.

The next morning, he invites the other leaders of the congregation to view the Motor, to see the slight pulsation that grows inside it. They listen attentively, but Spear sees the horror on their faces as he tries to point out the movement of the magnets again and again, as he grows frustrated at their inability to see what he sees. They leave at once, and Spear stands at the top of the hill, listening to their voices arguing on the way down the crooked path. By evening, their deliberations are complete, and when the messenger arrives at the cabin with a letter, Spear knows what it says before he reads it: He has been stripped of his position in the church, and of the church's material support.

Spear locks himself in the shed with the Motor, where he watches it pulsate through the night until morning, when there is a knock at the door. He opens the door to find Maud waiting for him. She is beautiful, transformed by her pregnancy, and she takes him by the hand, saying, This machine is ours to believe in, ours to take to the people.

She says, I have listened to your sermons, and I have heard the words you've spoken.

She says, You cannot give up. I won't allow it.

Spear nods, straightens himself and looks back at the machine he's built. There is life in it, he knows. He looks at Maud's hand in his. It is but a spark, but one day it will be a fire, if only he nurtures it.

There is no more money to pay for what Spear needs—wagons and assistants, supplies for the great journey ahead—and so Spear splits his time between the shed and his desk, between preparing for the disassembly of the Motor and writing letters begging for financial support. He writes to New York and Boston and Philadelphia and Washington, asking their spiritualist congregations to trust him, to help fund this new age that is coming.

He writes, The Glory of God is at hand, and soon I will bring it to each and every one of you, if only you will help me in these darkest of hours.

The words he writes, they are his alone, and he finds himself at a loss to explain the New Motor without the help of the Electricizers. He calls out to them, begs them for assistance.

In his empty office, he cries out, All that you helped me create is crumbling. Why won't you tell me what to write?

His words are met with silence, as they have been since the birth of the Motor. The Electricizers are no longer distinct to him, just blurred specters at the periphery of his vision, fading more every day. Their abandonment is near complete when Maud begins to help him instead, comforting his anxiety and giving him strength with her words. She has not gone down the hill since the day she gave birth, and Spear knows that this is the reason his family had to leave, that his congregation had to abandon him. Even the Electricizers leaving him, he recognizes it not as an abandonment but as making room for what is to come next.

Like Mary and Joseph's flight with the newborn Jesus into Egypt, he and Maud will flee with the New Motor across America, taking it by railroad to town after town after town.

Like Mary, Maud will not love him, only the Motor she has birthed.

Like Joseph, he will have to learn to live with this new arrangement, this adjusted set of expectations.

Spear tears up all the letters he has written so far, then starts new ones, ones infused not with the bitterness he feels but with the hope and inspiration he wishes he felt instead. Soon, the Motor will begin to speak to him, and he must be ready to listen.

It takes a month for the letters to come back, but Spear receives the responses he requires. He runs into the cabin, where Maud awaits him. He says, They're coming to help us, with money and with men. They'll be waiting for us in Randolph, ready to assist me in reassembling the Motor.

He hesitates, then says, I'll start tonight. I'll disassemble the Motor, and get it ready for travel, and then I'll send word to Randolph for a wagon to transport it. The worst is nearly over, and soon our new day will begin.

Maud rises from the dining table and takes Spear in her arms, cradling his head against her shoulder. She does not tell him what the angels have told her about what must happen instead, about what has always happened to those who have served God with hearts like his, too full of human weakness, of pride and folly and blinding hubris. She does not tell him about Moses at the border of the promised land, about Jonah in the belly of the whale. She could, but she chooses otherwise, chooses to repay his one-time lack of faith with her own.

Despite his intentions to start immediately, Spear finds that he cannot. Once he has locked himself in the shed with the New Motor, he is too in awe of its ornate existence, of the shining results of all the months of effort and prophecy that went into its construction. He watches the pulsation of the magnets and tries to understand what they might mean, what message might be hidden in their infant energies. He doesn't know, but he believes it will be made clear soon, even without the Electricizers' help.

Spear sits down on the floor of the shed and crosses his legs beneath him, preparing for the first time in many months to go into a trance, to purposefully pierce the shroud between this world and the next. The trance comes easily to him, in all of its usual ways: a prickling of the skin, a slowing of the breath, a blurring of the vision. He stays that way for many hours, listening, and so he does not hear the knock at the door, or the raised voices that follow. By the time something does snap him out of his trance—the first axe blow that bursts open the shed door, perhaps—it is far too late to save himself.

The men of the village surround him, swear they have come only to help him, to set him free of this thing he's made. Men who were once Spear's friends promise they won't hurt him, if only he'll lie still, but he can't, won't, not in the face of what they've come to do. Held between the arms of the two Russians, he watches disbelieving as one of High Rock's deacons steps to the New Motor, emboldened by the encouragement of the others. The deacon reaches up toward the grand revolver and takes hold of one of the magnetic spheres suspended from its crossbeams, and then he rips it away from the Motor.

Spear waits for intercession, for Electricizer or angel to step in and stop the destruction, but none appears. He struggles against his attackers, tries to warn them against what they plan to do, against the wrath of God they call down upon themselves, but they do not listen. Eventually he twists free and attempts to take a step toward the Motor, where others have joined the deacon in dismantling the hanging magnets. The Russians stop him, knock him to the ground, fall upon him with fists and boots, and when they tire of striking him they step aside so that others might have their turn. Spear no longer cares for himself, only for his new god, for this mechanical child gifted not just to him and to Maud, but also to all of mankind, if only they would accept it.

By the time Maud arrives in the doorway to the shed, he is already broken, in body and face and in spirit. The motor is crushed too, axe blows and wrenching hands tearing its intricate parts from their moorings, rendering meaningless the many names of God written in copper and zinc across its components. He cries to her for help, but knows there's nothing she can do. All around him are the men he once called to himself, who followed him to High Rock and up its steep hill to this shed, where he had meant for them to change their world. He watches the Russians and James the metalworker and the carpenters, all of them striking him or else the machine they themselves built. When they finish, when his teeth and bones are already shattered, he sees Randall, the youth he once admired above all others, and he lowers his head and accepts the vengeance the boy feels he's owed.

Before the beating ends, Spear lifts his head to look up at Maud, to take in her restored youth and beauty. For the last time, he sees the Electricizers, sees Jefferson and Franklin and Rush and Murray and all the others assembled around her. He cries out to them for protection, for salvation, and when they do not come to his aid he looks past them to Maud, who glows in their light, but also with a light of her own, something he wishes he had seen earlier, when there was still some great glory that might have come of it.

HER ENNEAD

Her baby is a joke, just a tiny bundle of cells dividing, too small to be taken seriously. For another week or two, it will still be smaller than the benign tumor she had removed from her breast two years ago, a realization that leads to her touching the place where that lump once was whenever she's alone. She jokes about this to her friends, who don't find it funny. She doesn't either, but she can't stop herself from sharing about her tumor-sized baby, growing and growing and growing, taking over her body. This time, no one wants her to stop it or get rid of it. This time, people say congratulations and hug her instead of pretending she's contagious, instead of forgetting her number until they hear she's better. Like before, she's only angry because everyone always assumes they already know exactly how she feels about the events that happen to her. She is careful to keep her true feelings to herself, to see that, as with the tumor, there is much she could lose.

Her baby is a seed, barely planted but already pushing roots through its waxy coat, searching for the dank soil it needs to grow inside her. She pictures it flowering but knows it'll be years before her baby is old enough for flowers, for seeds of its own. Her doctor emphasizes nutrition, suggests she drink six to eight glasses of water every day. She doesn't respond, doesn't tell him how many more she's already drinking. At home, she holds her face under the faucet, her throat pried open to swallow all the water she can. When she stands, her face and neck and shirt are soaked through, but it is not enough. She puts her lips back to the flowing water and drinks as deep as she can, as deep as she knows she must.

Her baby is a stone, and she wonders, How can I love a stone? It is cool and dark, something formed not in an instant—as she always assumed her baby would be—but instead over an age, an epoch. Everything about this feels slower than she'd imagined it would. She pictures her stone skipping across the hidden darkness of a lake, each point of contact a ripple expanding and then disappearing. She practices skipping stones herself while she waits for the baby to come, transforming every ditch and puddle and pond and lake into a microcosm, into a point of departure, a possible place where one day she will have to let go.

Her baby is a thunderstorm, a bundle of negatively and positively charged ions about to interact violently. It is a hurricane or a monsoon or a tsunami, but she doesn't know which, doesn't know how to tell the difference. She feels it churning inside, growing stronger with each revolution. Her levees will not hold. What happens after the baby comes will be different than what happened before. Whole countries she once knew will be swept away, their inhabitants scattered and replaced by new citizens, by other mothers and other children she has not yet met but in whose company she knows she will spend the rest of her life.

* * *

Her baby is a bird, mottled with gray and brown feathers that will last only as long as its infancy, when it will molt into splendor. Its mouth is open wide, waiting expectantly. Sometimes when she lies still in her quiet apartment, she can hear cawing from her round belly. She has cravings, contemplates eating quarters, little bits of tin foil, even a pair of silver earrings. She hopes her baby is building a beautiful nest inside of her. She wants to give it everything it needs so that it might never leave. Nest as lie, as false hope. Her baby is a bird of prey, something she has never been this close to before. All those talons. All that beak. It hooks her, devours her. They're both so hungry. She eats and eats. Before this, she never knew birds had tongues.

Her baby is a knife. A dagger. A broadsword, sharp and terrible. Her baby is a dangerous thing and she knows that if she isn't careful then one day it will hurt her, hurt others. When it kicks, she feels its edges pressed against the walls of its sheath, drawing more blood in a sea of blood. She is careful when she walks not to bump into things, not to put herself in harm's way. She wonders how it will hurt to push it from her body, to have the doctor tug her baby out of her as from a stone.

Her baby is a furred thing, alternately bristled and then soft. She hopes it isn't shedding, wonders how she'll ever get all that hair out of her if it is. She searches online for images of badgers and then wolverines, looking for something to recognize in their faces. She types the words *creatures that burrow*, then adds a question mark and tries again. The baby is so warm inside her, curled in on itself, waiting for winter to end, for a day to come when all the breath it's been holding can finally be expelled, like heat fogging the air of a still cold morning. Sometimes, when the baby rolls over and makes itself known, she can almost smell it.

Now the water breaking. Now the dilation of the cervix. Now the first real contraction, more potent than any of the false warnings she experienced before. Now the worry that this is too early, that she hasn't learned yet what her baby is supposed to be. Now the lack of thought and the loss of discernible time. Now the pain, which is sharp and dull and fast and slow, which is both waves and particles at the same time. Now the hurry, the burst into motion after the near year of waiting. Now the push, the pushing, the rushing stretch of her suddenly elastic body expanding to do this thing, to give birth to this baby. Now the joke, the seed, the stone, the storm, the bird, the sword. Now the tiny mammal, warm-blooded and hot and yes, now the head covered in wet hair. Now the shoulders, now the torso and the arms. Now the hipbones and the thighs and the knees and the feet. Now the first breath. Now the eyes opening. Now the cry, calling out to her like déjà vu, like the recognition of someone from a dream.

Now the baby.

Now the baby.

Now the baby, an event repeating for the rest of her life.

* * *

Her baby is a boy. Her baby is a girl. Her baby is potential energy changing to kinetic, is a person gaining momentum. Her baby is a possibility, or, rather, a string of possibilities and potentialities stretching forward from her toward something still unknowable. With the baby in her arms, she smiles. She coos. She tells her baby that it can be whatever it wants to be. She tells her baby that no matter what it turns out to be, she will always recognize it when it comes back to her. There is no shape that could hide her baby from her, no form that would make her turn her back on it. She says this like a promise, swears it like she can make it true, like it's just that easy. Some days, no matter what she says, her baby cries and cries and cries.

HOLD ON TO YOUR VACUUM

According to Teacher, there is only one rule, and it is this: No matter what happens, hold on to your vacuum. We have each been given one, each a different shape and size according to our needs. My own vacuum is bright red and bulky, as heavy as a ten-year-old, its worn cord slipping through my fingers like the tail of a rodent, thick and rubbery and repugnant. I start to complain, but Teacher holds up a hand and silences me.

Teacher says, This is the vacuum that was assigned to you, and the only one you'll be allowed to play with.

I don't know this man's actual name or title, whether he's referee or judge or umpire, but he reminds me of the man who taught my eighth-grade science class. He has the same balding hair pulled into a ponytail, the same small gold crucifix earring, and when he smiles he shows the same small yellow teeth pocked by smoke and sweets. I only know he's in charge because he's the one standing on the stage of the auditorium while the rest of us wait in the front row below. Because he's the only one of us without a vacuum of his own.

After my complaint, there are no other questions, and so Teacher says, I promise to count to at least one hundred before I come looking for you.

He says, I promise to look for you as long as you need me to, and then he says, Go.

* * *

As soon as Teacher finishes talking, the other players reach for their own vacuum cleaners and lug them up the aisle stairs, then out of the auditorium and into the lobby. From there, some move further into the building and some through the double glass doors into the world waiting outside, but why each person chooses one or the other is unclear to me. One girl is tall and thin and agile, her tiny hand vac fitting perfectly into her grip as she bounds out the door and across the parking lot. I follow her as far as the sidewalk, my hand resting on top of my own vacuum. Watching her run, I don't know where I should go or what I should do. This is only the first turn, and although Teacher has explained that the game is like hide and seek, I don't yet understand. I don't know what the rewards are for success, or what the punishment for failure might be.

I blink once and then Teacher is behind me. Before I can move, his arm shoots around my neck and pulls me into a wrestler's headlock, his grip strong and sure. His lips are beside my ear, the hairs of his moustache and beard tickling my face as he says, I thought I told you to run.

As he says, You're too stupid to be brave, so why didn't you run?

When his other hand comes into view, there is a cordless drill in its grip. The drill is matte black and dull yellow, loaded with a foot-long bit spinning at full speed. Teacher cocks my head and angles the drill downward into the crown of my skull. He pushes it in, past skin and bone, and then I scream and then I can't remember why I'm screaming and then I'm gone.

* * *

I'm carrying the vacuum again, trudging across a farm field full of snow toward the other side, where several rows of dark trees clumped between the snow and the cloudy sky might hide my red vacuum from the exposure of the open field. My lungs burn and my arms ache but I never question the necessity of lugging the vacuum everywhere I go. It is the only rule and so I follow it.

Once beneath the trees, I drag the vacuum over the blanketing floor of pine needles. Heading deeper into the woods, I find a tight bunch of pines whose boughs create a natural shelter into which I tuck myself and my vacuum. I expect to be hidden, to be safe, but I am not alone.

On the ground at my feet is a wounded deer, surrounded by a bloody halo of snow originating from the bullet hole tunneled through its chest. Rather than let go of the vacuum, I transfer its handle to my right hand as I kneel beside the deer. There is a knife in the snow, and because I don't know what else to do, I pick it up and hold it, looking over at the deer's still form, at the steam still rising from its blood. I think I know what I am supposed to do, but I don't know if I can do it.

I place the knife against the breastbone but can't bring myself to make the cut. I try again and fail again. This is why I never went hunting with my father or my brothers, at least not after the first time. I turn away, leaving the deer and the knife where I found them. When I step out from the press of the tree branches, Teacher's waiting for me, a thin smile on his face.

He says, You weren't able to do it before either, so nothing to feel bad about.

Then there is the drill. Then there is the end of my turn.

A new turn begins, in a high school locker room where I'm surrounded by other players, three boys in nothing but boxer shorts with vacuums of their own, giant shop vacs, low and squat on squeaky wheels. I'm naked before them, one hand on my vacuum and one on my crotch.

The biggest of the boys says, Want to get to your locker, don't you?

Probably pretty ashamed of that little prick. Needs to put his panties on.

Show us what you've got and I'll let you pass. I promise.

This boy, his vacuum is bigger than the others, and also an unmistakable hue of pink.

I know he's not telling the truth. Whatever happens, someone is definitely going to get hurt.

The boys continue to taunt me, and right before I know I'm about to give in, to just get it over with, the door to the locker room slams open, and in comes Teacher. He smiles, all his little crowded teeth gleaming victorious in the fluorescence.

We scatter, but he's too fast, the scene too disorienting. The drill enters the bullies first, but eventually it comes for me too.

There is a turn where my father bails me out of jail and then there is the drill. Where my mother finds my slim pornography stash, the drill coming as she tells me who it was that molested her and how she's afraid I'm going to grow up to be like him. I call a boy in the second grade a nigger even though I don't know what the word means. The drill enters through my cheek so that I can feel it spinning inside my mouth before it angles upward toward my brain. These turns I never hear Teacher coming, never see him except as a hand holding a weapon.

The line between voyeur and participant blurs. I open a bathroom door and see my babysitter partially naked, squatting with her pants around her ankles, changing her tampon. This is years before I even know what that is. I back out quickly, yelling apologies, my vacuum clunking against the doorframe. Later I will reenact an early masturbation attempt, one hand on myself and the other on the vacuum's handle as I picture the triangle of pubic hair between her legs. The drill bit finds me right before I orgasm. It is a long time before I see another player again, and when I do I can't help wondering if I'm playing against them or beside them, if we are rivals or on the same team. It's hard to know. My only companion comes via the one rule: *Hold on to your vacuum.* It goes everywhere with me, a conjoined twin or else a tumor made of Chinese plastic and rubber belts.

I grow calmer, more accepting of the drill, like a child who learns to take his medicine no matter how bad it tastes: I'm in a house, behind Teacher now, stalking him for once. A new kind of turn. Teacher climbs a staircase, seemingly unaware of my presence behind him. At the top of the stairs, he enters the first room on the left and closes the door behind him. I follow, dragging the red vacuum as quietly as possible. I don't have the strength anymore to lift it over the stairs, but I do drag it as quietly as possible, easing it over the carpeted hump of each step. At the top, I remember an old trick I used to play on my younger siblings. I tie one end of my vacuum cord around the handle of the door Teacher's behind, one to the closed door across the hall. When I open the door on the other side and lower its doorstop, it pulls the cord tight, making it impossible to move either door. I stand in the hallway and wait for Teacher to try to escape. Fifteen minutes pass and still I resolve to be patient. I sit on the floor, cradling my vacuum, rocking it in my arms. It is heavy, far heavier than it was before, and it stinks of burning rubber and fried dust. Impatient, I press my ear against Teacher's door, listening, and by the time I hear the drill bit chewing through the door, it's too late to move. Not that I would. I cry out as the bit clears the wood and hits my temple, but only in relief. My hippocampus must be shredded wheat by now and still I crave more, more, more.

Most turns I'm somewhere I don't want to be, someplace I've been once and wouldn't willingly revisit. I'm a child, making up a story about a man trying to abduct me just to make my mother feel bad for leaving me in the car alone while she paid for her gas. The vacuum's on the floor of the car between my chubby little legs, Teacher's in the back seat cleaning his glasses. I come to the worst lie I ever told my wife and it is one of the lowest moments of my life. Even though she never thought to doubt me, it is still terrible living through it again.

Once in a while, the turns bring me to rarer moments, like my college graduation or my wedding day. Moments where my parents or friends or my wife told me they loved me and were proud of me. Moments where a handshake or a hug or a kiss is interrupted by the drill bit battering down the doors of my skull. These are the times I scream the loudest, that I struggle against the bit's insistence, but Teacher has the steady hand of a surgeon or else an assassin. Of all the players in the game, only he seems constantly sure of his role.

Now there is a turn that is fully recognizable as my own memory, turned into what I know is another game board, another level. I'm at a party when I'm eighteen or nineteen. Everyone is drunk, and everyone has their vacuum with them. I keep drinking, leaning against my vacuum for support, talking to a blonde girl in a miniskirt for hours. She tells me about her boyfriend who's away at school and I keep pressing, trying too hard but still we end up in a bedroom upstairs, both of us barely conscious, our vacuums leaned against the bed, our bodies tangled in their cords.

I kiss her and she says, I don't know about this.

I answer by kissing her again.

My hand moves under her skirt, the part of me that is playing the game mimicking the part of me that is a memory.

This is not something I think of often.

It is not something I've ever told anyone.

Here, in the game, I stop and pull my hand away. I say, I'm so sorry for what I did to you, and the girl doesn't say anything back because she's too far gone to talk.

I say, I promise I won't do it again, and then I get out of the bed, untangle our cords, and cover her gently with a blanket. When I walk downstairs to find her friends, to tell them they need to look after her, I see that the party is deserted, its falsehood revealed. The only person left is Teacher, holding his big black drill in one hand, a red plastic cup of beer in the other. When he stands and starts walking toward me, I step back, raise my hands in protest.

I say, It's over. There's nothing for you here. I changed what happened all by myself.

He moves quickly then, carelessly whipping his beer away in an arc of foam as his other hand shoots up and forward, shoving the drill at my face, the bit already whirling threats. He shakes his head, says, As if one moment was all it took.

I say, I'm still ashamed, Teacher. I'm just not afraid of my shame anymore.

I wrap my arms around the vacuum and its bag full of my dirt. Teacher pulls the trigger, but it is meaningless and he knows it. There are other rules besides the first one, and despite the drill I have begun to discover them.

No new turn follows, only some sort of timeout, intermission. I'm sitting in the end zone of a high school football field while sweat drips from my face, my arms and legs shaking from exertion. Even my vacuum looks tired, its belt worn, its bag full to the point of bursting. Teacher walks across the field with his drill dangling loosely in his grip, and while there's no malice in his movement, I can't help jerking away when he comes to sit beside me. The armpits of his shirt are darkened with sweat like sulfur and cheap cologne, rotten eggs soaked in musk.

He says, Why be afraid? Why resist? The only thing I'm killing are the places you were most scared, the places you were caught, found out for what you are.

That's not true, I say, thinking about the moments where I was proudest, where someone decided I was a good husband, a good son, a good friend. Memories rare enough before the drill.

Teacher smiles, more teeth than curved lips. He says, Good with the bad, sweet with the sour, sometimes you gotta amputate the heart to save the head.

And then there is the drill bit again, pressed against my forehead, already biting through.

I say, I don't want to play anymore.

I say, It's not fair to everyone I hurt if I can forget what I did to them.

The drill turns slowly, tearing the skin without piercing the bone beneath. The bit is both cold and hot at the same time. Half of my memories are gone, replaced with the dead nothingness of Teacher's treatment. If Teacher wins, there will be no remainder left behind.

Through the pain, I say, You cheated. You never explained the rest of the rules. You never told us there was a chance we could win too.

And then I see it, the solution, how to turn the half-life left to play into a second chance, the possibility of being better. I smile too now, wider than I have in all these sad years, and even with the drill twisting through my face I can see that Teacher is for a moment as afraid of me as I am of him.

Teacher says, You're the one who asked to play, and then he presses the red trigger the rest of the way. The drill bit slides through bone and brain all over again, but this time I don't give in as quickly. I focus, desperate to hold out for even one more millisecond than I have before. Even that will be an improvement, the first play at the beginning of a big comeback.

Teacher says, Game on, and as my eyes shut, I think, Yes, yes, it is.

DREDGE

The drowned girl drips everywhere, soaking the cheap cloth of the Ford's back seat. Punter stares at her from the front of the car, first taking in her long blond hair, wrecked by the pond's amphibian sheen, then her lips, blue where the lipstick's been washed away, flaky red where it has not. He looks into her glassy green eyes, her pupils so dilated the irises are slivered halos, the right eye further polluted with burst blood vessels. She wears a lace-frilled gold tank top, a pair of acid wash jeans with grass stains on the knees and the ankles. A silver bracelet around her wrist throws off sparkles in the window-filtered moonlight, the same sparkle he saw through the lake's dark mirror, that made him drop his fishing pole and wade out, then dive in after her. Her feet are bare except for a silver ring on her left pinkie toe, suggesting the absence of sandals, flip-flops, something lost in a struggle. Suggesting too many things for Punter to process all at once.

Punter turns and faces forward. He lights a cigarette, then flicks it out the window after just two drags. Smoking with the drowned girl in the car reminds him of when he worked at the plastics factory, how he would sometimes taste melted plastic in every puff of smoke. How a cigarette there hurt his lungs, left him gasping, his tongue coated with the taste of polyvinyl chloride, of adipates and phthalates. How that taste would leave his throat sore, would make his stomach ache all weekend.

The idea that some part of the dead girl might end up inside him—her wet smell or sloughing skin or dumb luck—he doesn't need a cigarette that bad.

Punter crawls halfway into the back seat and arranges the girl as comfortably as he can, while he still can. He's hunted enough deer and rabbits and squirrels to know she's going to stiffen soon. He arranges her arms and legs until she appears asleep, then brushes her hair out of her face before he climbs back into his own seat.

Looking in the rearview, Punter smiles at the drowned girl, waits for her to smile back. Feels his face flush when he remembers she's never going to.

He starts the engine. Drives her home.

Punter lives fifteen minutes from the pond but tonight it takes longer. He keeps the Ford five miles per hour under the speed limit, stops extra long at every stop sign. He thinks about calling the police, about how he should have already done so, instead of dragging the girl onto the shore and into his car.

The cops, they'll call this disturbing the scene of a crime. Obstructing justice. Tampering with evidence.

What the cops will say about what he's done, Punter already knows all about it.

At the house, he leaves the girl in the car while he goes inside and shits, his stool as black and bloody as it has been for months. It burns when he wipes. He needs to see a doctor, but doesn't have insurance, hasn't since getting fired.

Afterward, he sits at the kitchen table and smokes a cigarette. The phone is only a few feet away, hanging on the wall. Even though the service was disconnected a month ago, he's pretty sure he could still call 911, if he wanted to.

He doesn't want to.

In the garage, he lifts the lid of the chest freezer that sits against the far wall. He stares at the open space above the paper-wrapped bundles of venison, tries to guess if there's enough room, then stacks piles of burger and steak and sausage on the floor until he's sure. He goes out to the car and opens the back door. He lifts the girl, grunting as he gathers her into his arms like a child. He's not as strong as he used to be, and she's heavier than she looks, with all the water filling her lungs and stomach and intestinal tract. Even through her tank top he can see the way it bloats her belly like she's pregnant. He's careful as he lays her in the freezer, as he brushes the hair out of her eyes again, as he holds her eyelids closed until he's sure they'll stay that way.

The freezer will give him time to figure out what he wants. What he needs. What he and she are capable of together.

Punter wakes in the middle of the night and puts his boots on in a panic. In the freezer, the girl's covered in a thin layer of frost, and he realizes he shouldn't have put her away wet. He considers taking her out, thawing her, toweling her off, but doesn't. It's too risky. One thing Punter knows about himself is that he is not always good at saying when.

He closes the freezer lid, goes back to the house, back to bed but not to sleep. Even wide awake, he can see the curve of her neck, the interrupting line of her collarbones intersecting the thin straps of her tank top. He reaches under his pajama bottoms, past the elastic of his underwear, then squeezes himself until the pain takes the erection away.

On the news the next morning, there's a story about the drowned girl. The anchorman calls her missing but then says the words *her name was.* Punter winces. It's only a slip, but he knows how hurtful the past tense can be.

The girl is younger than Punter had guessed, a high school senior at the all-girls school across town. Her car was found yesterday, parked behind a nearby gas station, somewhere Punter occasionally fills up his car, buys cigarettes and candy bars.

The anchorman says the police are currently investigating, but haven't released any leads to the public.

The anchorman looks straight into the camera and says it's too early to presume the worst, that the girl could still show up at any time.

Punter shuts off the television, stubs out his cigarette. He takes a shower, shaves, combs his black hair straight back. Dresses himself in the same outfit he wears every day, a white t-shirt and blue jeans and black motorcycle boots.

On the way to his car, he stops by the garage and opens the freezer lid. Her body is obscured behind ice like frosted glass. He puts a finger to her lips, but all he feels is cold.

* * *

The gas station is on a wooded stretch of gravel road between Punter's house and the outskirts of town. Although Punter has been here before, he's never seen it so crowded. While he waits in line he realizes these people are here for the same reason he is, to be near the site of the tragedy, to see the last place this girl was seen.

The checkout line crawls while the clerk runs his mouth, ruining his future testimony by telling his story over and over, transforming his eyewitness account into another harmless story.

The clerk says, I was the only one working that night. Of course I remember her.

In juvie, the therapists had called this narrative therapy, or else constructing a preferred reality.

The clerk says, Long blond hair, tight-ass jeans, all that tan skin—I'm not saying she brought it on herself, but you can be sure she knew people would be looking.

The clerk, he has black glasses and halitosis and fingernails chewed to keratin pulp. Teeth stained with cigarettes or chewing tobacco or coffee. Or all of the above. He reminds Punter of himself, and he wonders if the clerk feels the same, if there is a mutual recognition between them.

When it's Punter's turn, the clerk says, I didn't see who took her, but I wish I had.

Punter looks away, reads the clerk's name tag.

OSWALD.

The clerk says, If I knew who took that girl, I'd kill him myself.

Punter shivers as he slides his bills across the counter, as he takes his carton of cigarettes and his candy bar. He doesn't stop shivering until he gets out of the air-conditioned store and back inside his sun-struck car.

The therapists had told Punter that what he'd done was a mistake, that there was nothing wrong with him. They made him repeat their words back to them, to absolve himself of the guilt they were so sure he was feeling.

The therapists had said, You were just kids. You didn't know what you were doing.

Punter said the words they wanted, but doing so changed nothing. He'd never felt the guilt they told him he should. Even now, he has only the remembered accusations of cops and judges to convince him that what he did was wrong.

Punter cooks two venison steaks in a frying pan with salt and butter. He sits down to eat, cuts big mouthfuls, then chews and chews, the meat tough from overcooking. He eats past the point of satiation on into discomfort, until his stomach presses against the tight skin of his abdomen. He never knows how much food to cook. He always clears his plate.

When he's done eating, he smokes and thinks about the girl in the freezer. How, when walking her out of the pond, she had threatened to slip out of his arms and back into the water. How he'd held on, carrying her up and out into the starlight. He hadn't saved her—couldn't have—but he had preserved her, kept her safe from the wet decay, from the mouths of fish and worse.

He knows the freezer is better than the refrigerator, that the dry cold of meat and ice is better than the slow rot of lettuce and leftovers and ancient, crust-rimmed condiments. Knows that even after death, there is a safety in the preservation of a body, that there is a second kind of life to be had.

Punter hasn't been to the bar near the factory since he got fired, but tonight he needs a drink. By eight, he's already been out to the garage four times, unable to keep from opening the freezer lid. If he doesn't stop, the constant thawing and refreezing will destroy her, skin first.

It's mid-shift at the factory, so the bar is empty except for the bartender and two men sitting together at the rail, watching the ball game on the television mounted above the liquor shelves. Punter takes a stool at the opposite end, orders a beer and lights a cigarette. He looks at the two men, tries to decide if they're men he knows from the plant. He's bad with names, bad at faces. One of the men catches him looking and gives him a glare that Punter immediately looks away from. He knows that he stares too long at people, that it makes them uncomfortable, but he can't help himself. He moves his eyes to his hands to his glass to the game, which he also can't make any sense of. Sports move too fast, are full of rules and behaviors he finds incomprehensible.

During commercials, the station plugs its own late-night newscast, including the latest about the missing girl. Punter stares at the picture of her on the television screen, his tongue growing thick and dry for the five seconds the image is displayed. One of the other men drains the last gulp of his beer and shakes his head, says, I hope they find the fucker that killed her and cut his balls off.

So you think she's dead then?

Of course she's dead. You don't go missing like that and not end up dead.

The men motion for another round as the baseball game comes back from the break. Punter realizes he's been holding his breath, lets it go in a loud, hacking gasp. The bartender and two men turn to look, so he holds a hand up, trying to signal he doesn't need any help, then puts it down when he realizes they're not offering. He pays his tab and gets up to leave.

He hasn't thought much about how the girl got into the pond, or who put her there. He too assumed murder, but the who or why or when is not something he's previously considered.

In juvie, the counselors told him nothing he did or didn't do would have kept his mother alive, which Punter understood fine. Of course he hadn't killed his mother. That wasn't why he was there. It was what he'd done afterward that had locked him away, put him behind bars until he was eighteen.

This time, he will do better. He won't sit around for months while the police slowly solve the case, while they decide that what he's done is just as bad. This time, Punter will find the murderer himself, and he will make him pay.

He remembers: Missing her. Not knowing where she was, not understanding, just wishing she'd come back. Not believing his father, who told him that she'd left them, that she was gone forever.

He remembers looking for her all day while his father worked, wandering the road, the fields, the rooms of their small house.

He remembers descending into the basement one step at a time. Finding the light switch, waiting for the fluorescent tubes to warm up. Stepping off the wood steps, his bare feet aching at the cold of the concrete floor.

He remembers nothing out of the ordinary, everything in its place.

He remembers the olive green refrigerator and the hum of the lights being the only two sounds in the world.

He remembers walking across the concrete and opening the refrigerator door.

More than anything else, he remembers opening his mouth to scream and not being able to. He remembers that scream getting trapped in his chest, never to emerge.

When the eleven o' clock news comes on, Punter is watching, ready with his small, spiral-bound notebook and his golf pencil stolen from the keno caddy at the bar. He writes down the sparse information added to the girl's story. The reporter recounts what Punter already knows—her name, the school, the abandoned car—then plays a clip of the local sheriff, who leans into the reporter's microphone and says, We're still investigating, but so far there's no proof for any of these theories. It's rare when someone gets out of their car and disappears on their own, but it does happen.

The sheriff pauses, listening to an inaudible question, then says, Whatever happened to her, it didn't happen inside the car. There's no sign of a struggle, no sign of sexual assault or worse.

Punter crosses his legs, then uncrosses them. He presses the pencil down onto the paper and writes all of this down.

The next clip is of the girl's father and mother, standing behind a podium at a press conference. They are both dressed in black, both stern and sad in dress clothes. The father speaks, saying, If anyone out there knows what happened—if you know where our daughter is—please come forward. We need to know where she is.

Punter writes down the word *father*, writes down the words *mother* and *daughter*. He looks at his useless telephone. He could tell these strangers what they wanted, but what good would it do them? His own father had known exactly where his mother was, and it hadn't done either of them any good.

According to the shows on television, the first part of an investigation is always observation, is always the gathering of clues. Punter opens the closet where he keeps his hunting gear and takes his binoculars out of their case. He hangs them around his neck and closes the closet door, then reopens it and takes his hunting knife off the top shelf. He doesn't need it, not yet, but he knows television detectives always carry a handgun to protect themselves. He only owns a rifle and a shotgun, both too long for this kind of work. The knife will have to be enough.

In the car, he puts the knife in the glove box and the binoculars on the seat. He takes the notebook out of his back pocket and reads the list of locations he's written down: the school, her parents' house, the pond and the gas station.

He reads the time when the clerk said he saw her and then writes down another, the time he found her in the pond. The two times are separated by barely a day, so she couldn't have been in the pond for too long.

Whatever happened to her, it happened fast.

He thinks that whoever did this, they must be a local to know about the pond. Punter has never actually seen anyone else there, only the occasional tire tracks, the left-behind beer bottles and cigarette butts from teenage parties. The condoms discarded further off in the bushes, where Punter goes to piss.

He thinks about the girl, about how he knows she would never consent to him touching her if she were still alive. About how she would never let him say the words he's said, the words he still wants to say. He wonders what he will do when he finds her killer. His investigation, it could be either an act of vengeance or thanksgiving, but it is still too early to know which.

Punter has been to the girl's school once before, when the unemployment office sent him to interview for a janitorial position there. He hadn't been offered the job, couldn't have passed the background check if he had. His juvenile record was sealed, but there was enough there to warn people, and schools never took any chances.

He circles the parking lot twice, then parks down the sidewalk from the front entrance, where he'll be able to watch people coming in and out of the school. He resists the urge to use the binoculars, knows he must control himself in public, must keep from acting on every thought he has. This is why he hasn't talked in months. Why he keeps to himself in his house, hunting and fishing, living off the too-small government disability checks the unemployment counselors helped him apply for.

These counselors, they hadn't wanted him to see what they wrote down for his disability, but he had. Seeing those words written in the counselor's neat script didn't make him angry, just relieved to know. He wasn't bad anymore. He was a person with a disorder, with a trauma. No one had ever believed him about this, especially not the therapist in juvie, who had urged Punter to open up, who had gotten angry when he couldn't. They didn't believe him when he said he'd already told them everything he had inside him.

Punter knows they were right to disbelieve him, that he did have feelings he didn't want to let out.

When Punter pictures the place where other people keep their feelings, all he sees is his own trapped scream, imagined as a devouring ball of sound, hungry and hot in his guts.

A bell rings from inside the building. Soon the doors open, spilling girls out onto the sidewalk and into the parking lot. Punter watches parents getting out of other cars, going to greet their children. One of these girls might be a friend of the drowned girl, and if he could talk to her then he might be able to find out who the drowned girl was. Might be able to make a list of other people he needed to question so that he could solve her murder.

The volume and the increasing number of distinct voices, all of it overwhelms Punter. He stares, watching the girls go by in their uniforms. All of them are identically clothed and so he focuses instead on their faces, on their hair, on the differences between blondes and brunettes and redheads. He watches the girls smiling and rolling their eyes and exchanging embarrassed looks as their mothers step forward to receive them.

He watches the breeze blow all that hair around all those made-up faces. He presses himself against the closed door of his Ford, holds himself still.

He closes his eyes and tries to picture the drowned girl here, wearing her own uniform, but she is separate now, distinct from these girls and the life they once shared. Punter's glad. These girls terrify him in a way the drowned girl does not.

A short burst of siren startles Punter, and he twists around in his seat to see a police cruiser idling its engine behind him, its driver side window rolled down. The cop inside is around Punter's age, his hair starting to gray at the temples but the rest of him young and healthy-looking. The cop yells something, hanging his left arm out the window, drumming his fingers against the side of the cruiser, but Punter can't hear him through the closed windows, not with all the other voices surrounding him.

Punter opens his mouth, then closes it without saying anything. He shakes his head, then locks his driver's side door, suddenly afraid that the cop means to drag him from the car, to put hands on him as other officers did when he was a kid. He looks up from the lock to see the cop outside of his cruiser, walking toward Punter's own car.

The cop raps on Punter's window, waits for him to roll down the window. He stares at Punter, who tries to look away, inadvertently letting his eyes fall on another group of teenage girls.

The cop says, You need to move your car. This is a fire lane.

Punter tries to nod, finds himself shaking his head instead. He whispers that he'll leave, that he's leaving. The cop says, I can't hear you. What did you say?

Punter turns the key, sighs when the engine turns over. He says, I'm going. He says it as loud as he can, his vocal cords choked and rusty.

There are too many girls walking in front of him for Punter to pull forward, and so he has to wait as the cop gets back in his own car. Eventually the cop puts the cruiser in reverse, lets him pass. Punter drives slowly out of the parking lot and onto the city streets, keeping the car slow, keeping it straight between the lines.

Afraid that the cop might follow him, Punter sticks to the main roads, other well-populated areas, but he gets lost anyway. These aren't places he goes. A half hour passes, and then another. Punter's throat is raw from smoking. His eyes ache from staring into the rearview mirror, and his hands tremble so long he fears they might never stop.

At home, Punter finds the girl's parents in the phonebook, writes down their address. He knows he has to be more careful, that if he isn't then someone will come looking for him too. He lies down on the couch to wait for dark, falls asleep with the television tuned to daytime dramas and court shows. He dreams about finding the murderer, about hauling him into the police station in chains. He sees himself avenging the girl with a smoking pistol, emptying round after round into this faceless person, unknown but certainly out there, surely as marked by his crime as Punter was.

When he wakes up, the television is still on, broadcasting game shows full of questions Punter isn't prepared to answer. He gets up and goes into the bathroom, the pain in his guts doubling him over on the toilet. When he's finished, he takes a long, gulping drink from the faucet, then goes out into the living room to gather his notebook, his binoculars, his knife.

In the garage, he tries to lift the girl's tank top to get to the skin hidden underneath, but the fabric is frozen to her flesh. He can't tell if the sound of his efforts is the ripping of ice or of skin. He tries touching her through her clothes, but she's too far gone, distant with cold. He shuts the freezer door and leaves her again in the dark, but not before he explains what he's doing for her. Not before he promises to find the person who hurt her, to hurt this person himself.

Her parents' house is outside of town, at the end of a long tree-lined driveway. Punter drives past, then leaves his car parked down the road and walks back with the binoculars around his neck. Moving through the shadows of the trees, he finds a spot a hundred yards from the house, then scans the lighted windows for movement until he finds the three figures sitting in the living room. He recognizes her parents from the television, sees that the third person is a boy around the same age as the drowned girl. Punter watches him the closest, tries to decide if this is the girl's boyfriend. The boy is all movement, his hands gesturing with every word he speaks. He could be laughing or crying or screaming and from this distance Punter wouldn't be able to tell the difference. He watches as the parents embrace the boy, then hurries back through the woods as soon as he sees the headlights come on in front of the house.

He makes it to his own car just as the boy's convertible pulls out onto the road. Punter starts the engine and follows the convertible through town, past the gas station and the downtown shopping, then into another neighborhood where the houses are smaller. He's never been here before, but he knows the plastics plant is close, that many of his old coworkers live nearby. He watches the boy park in front of a dirty white house, watches through the binoculars as the boy climbs the steps to the porch, as he rings the doorbell. The boy does not go in, but Punter's view is still obscured by the open door. Whatever happens only takes a few minutes, and then the boy is back in his car. He sits on the side of the road for a long time, smoking. Punter smokes too. He imagines getting out of the car and going up to the boy, imagines questioning him about the night of the murder. He knows he should, knows being a detective means taking risks, but he can't do it. When the boy leaves, Punter lets him go, then drives past the white house with his foot off the gas pedal, idling at a crawl. He doesn't see anything he understands, but this is not exactly new.

Back at the pond, the only evidence he gathers is that he was there himself. His tire tracks are the only ones backing up to the pond, his footprints the only marks along the shore. Whoever else was there before him has been given an alibi by Punter's own clumsiness.

He knows how this will look, so he finds a long branch with its leaves intact and uses it to rake out the sand, erasing the worst of his tracks. When he's done, he stares out over the dark water, trying to remember how it felt to hold her in his arms, to feel her body soft and pliable before surrendering her to the freezer.

He wonders if it was a mistake to take her from beneath the water. Maybe he should have done the opposite, should have stayed under the waves with her until his own lungs filled with the same watery weight, until he was trapped beside her. Their bodies would not have lasted. The fish would have dismantled their shells, and then Punter could have shown her the good person he's always believed himself to be, trapped underneath all this sticky rot.

For dinner he cooks two more steaks. All the venison the girl displaced is going bad in his aged refrigerator, and already the steaks are browned and bruised. To be safe, he fries them hard as leather. He has to chew the venison until his jaws ache and his teeth feel loose, but he finishes every bite, not leaving behind even the slightest scrap of fat.

Watching the late night news, Punter can tell that without any new evidence the story is losing steam. The girl gets only a minute of coverage, the reporter reiterating facts Punter's known for days. He stares at her picture again, at how her smile once made her whole face seem alive.

He knows he doesn't have much time. He crawls toward the television on his hands and knees, puts his hand on her image as it fades away. He turns around, sits with his back against the television screen. Behind him there is satellite footage of a tornado or a hurricane or a flood. Of destruction seen from afar.

Punter wakes up choking in the dark, his throat closed off with something, phlegm or pus or he doesn't know what. He grabs a handkerchief from his nightstand and spits over and over until he clears away the worst of it. He gets up to flip the light switch, but the light doesn't turn on. He tries it again, and then once more. He realizes how quiet the house is, how without the steady clacking of his wall clock the only sound in his bedroom is his own thudding heart. He leaves the bedroom, walks into the kitchen. The oven's digital clock stares at him like an empty black eye, the refrigerator waits silent and still.

He runs out of the house in his underwear, his big bare feet slapping at the cold driveway. Inside the garage, the freezer is silent too. He lifts the lid, letting out a blast of frozen air, then slams it shut again after realizing he's wasted several degrees of chill to confirm something he already knows.

He knew this day was coming—the power company has given him ample written notice—but still he curses in frustration. He goes back inside and dresses hurriedly, then scavenges his house for loose change, for crumpled dollar bills left in discarded jeans. At the grocery down the road, he buys what little ice he can afford, his cash reserves exhausted until his next disability check. It's not enough, but it's all he can do.

Back in the garage, he works fast, cracking the blocks of ice on the cement floor and dumping them over the girl's body. He manages to cover her completely, suppressing the pang of regret he feels once he's unable to see her face through the ice. For a second, he considers crawling inside the freezer himself, sweeping away the ice between them. Letting his body heat hers, letting her thaw into his arms.

What he wonders is, Would it be better to have one day with her than a forever separated by ice?

He goes back into the house and sits down at the kitchen table. Lights a cigarette, then digs through the envelopes on the table until he finds the unopened bill from the power company. He opens it, reads the impossible number, shoves the bill back into the envelope. He tries to calculate how long the ice will buy him, but he never could do figures, can't begin to start to solve a problem like this.

He remembers: The basement refrigerator had always smelled bad, like leaking coolant and stale air. It wasn't used much, had been kept out of his father's refusal to throw anything away more than out of any sense of utility. By the time Punter found his mother there, she was already bloated around the belly and the cheeks, her skin slick with something that glistened like petroleum jelly.

Unsure what he should do, he'd slammed the refrigerator door and ran back upstairs to hide in his bedroom. By the time his father came home, Punter was terrified his father would know he'd seen, that he'd kill him too. That what would start as a beating would end as a murder.

Only his father never said anything, never gave any sign the mother was dead. He stuck to his story, telling Punter over and over how his mother had run away and left them behind, until Punter's voice was too muted to ask.

Punter tried to forget, to believe his father's story, but he couldn't.

Punter tried to tell someone else, some adult, but he couldn't do that either. Not when he knew what would happen to his father. Not when he knew they would take her from him.

During the day, while his father worked, he went down to the basement and opened the refrigerator door.

At first, he only looked at her, at the open eyes and mouth, at the way her body had been jammed into the too-small space. At the way her throat was slit the same way his dad had once demonstrated on a deer that had fallen but not expired.

The first time he touched her, he was sure she was trying to speak to him, but it was only gas leaking out of her mouth, squeaking free of her lungs. Punter had rushed to pull her out of the refrigerator, convinced for a moment she was somehow alive, but when he wrapped his arms around her, all that gas rolled out of her mouth and nose and ears, sounding like a wet fart but smelling so much worse.

He hadn't meant to vomit on her, but he couldn't help himself.

Afterward, he took her upstairs and bathed her to get the puke off. He'd never seen another person naked, and so he tried not to look at his mother's veiny breasts, at the wet thatch of her pubic hair floating in the bath water.

Scrubbing her with a washcloth and a bar of soap, he averted his eyes the best he could.

Rinsing the shampoo out of her hair, he whispered he was sorry.

It was hard to dress her, but eventually he managed, and then it was time to put her back in the refrigerator before his father came home.

Closing the door, he whispered goodbye. I love you. I'll see you tomorrow.

The old clothes, covered with blood and vomit, he took them out into the cornfield behind the house and buried them. Then came the waiting, all through the evening while his father occupied the living room, all through the night while he was supposed to be sleeping.

Day after day, he took her out and wrestled her up the stairs. He sat her on the couch or at the kitchen table, and then he talked, his normal reticence somehow negated by her forever silence. He'd never talked to his mother this much while she was alive, but now he couldn't stop telling her everything he had ever felt, all his trapped words spilling out one after another.

Punter knows that even if they hadn't found her and taken her away, she wouldn't have lasted forever. He had started finding little pieces of her left behind, waiting wet and squishy on the wooden basement steps, the kitchen floor, in between the cracks of the couch.

He tried to clean up after her, but sometimes his father would find one too. Then Punter would have to watch as his father held some squishy flake up to the light, rolling it between his fingers as if he could not recognize what it was or where it came from before throwing it in the trash.

Day after day, Punter bathed his mother to get rid of the smell, which grew more pungent as her face began to droop, as the skin on her arms wrinkled and sagged. He searched her body for patches of mold to scrub them off, then held her hands in his, marveling at how, even weeks later, her fingernails continued to grow.

Punter sits on his front step, trying to make sense of the scribbles in his notebook. He doesn't have enough, isn't even close to solving the crime, but he knows he has to, if he wants to keep the police away. If they figure the crime out before he does, if they question the killer, then they'll eventually end up at the pond, where Punter's attempts at covering his tracks are unlikely to be good enough.

Punter doesn't need to prove the killer guilty, at least not with a judge and a jury. All he has to do is find this person, then make sure he never tells anyone what he did with the body. After that, the girl can be his forever, for as long as he has enough ice.

Punter drives, circling the scenes of the crime: The gas station, the school, her parents' house, the pond. He drives the circuit over and over, and even with the air conditioning cranked he can't stop sweating, his face drenched and fevered, his stomach hard with meat. He's halfway between his house and the gas station when his gas gauge hits empty. He pulls over and sits for a moment, trying to decide, trying to wrap his slow thoughts around his investigation. He opens his notebook, flips through its barely filled pages. He has written down so few facts, so few suspects, and there is so little time left.

In his notebook, he crosses out *father, mother, boyfriend*. He has only one name left, one suspect he hasn't disqualified, one other person that Punter knows has seen the girl. He smokes, considers, tries to prove himself right or wrong, gets nowhere.

He opens the door and stands beside the car. Home is in one direction, the gas station the other. Reaching back inside, he leaves the notebook and the binoculars but takes the hunting knife and shoves it into his waistband, untucking his t-shirt to cover the weapon.

What Punter decides, he knows it is only a guess, but he also believes that whenever a detective has a hunch, the best thing to do is to follow it to the end.

It's not a long walk, but Punter gets tired fast. He sits down to rest, then can't get back up. He curls into a ball off the weed-choked shoulder, sleeps fitfully as cars pass by, their tires throwing loose gravel over his body. It's dark out when he wakes. His body is covered with gray dust, and he can't remember where he is. He's never walked this road before, and in the dark it's as alien as a foreign land. He studies the meager footprints in the dust, tracking himself until he knows which way he needs to go.

There are two cars parked behind the gas station, where the drowned girl's car was before it was towed away. One is a small compact, the other a newer sports car. The sports car's windows are rolled down, its stereo blaring music Punter doesn't know or understand, the words too fast for him to hear. He takes a couple steps into the trees beside the road, slows his approach until his gasps for air grow quieter. Leaning against the station are two young men in t-shirts and blue jeans, nearly identical with their purposely mussed hair and scraggly stubble. With them are two girls—one redhead and one brunette—still wearing their school uniforms, looking even younger than Punter knows they are.

The brunette presses her hand against her man's chest, and the man's own hand clenches her hip. Punter can see how firmly he's holding her, how her skirt is bunched between his fingers, exposing several extra inches of thigh.

He thinks of his girl thawing at home, how soon he will have to decide how badly he wants to feel that, to feel her skin so close to his own.

He thinks of the boyfriend he saw through the binoculars. Wonders if *boyfriend* is really the word he needs.

The redhead, she takes something from the unoccupied man, puts it on her tongue. The man laughs, then motions to his friend, who releases his girl and picks a twelve pack of beer up off the cement. All four of them get into the sports car and drive off together in the direction of the pond, the town beyond. Punter stands still as they pass, knowing they won't see him, that he is already—has always been—a ghost to their world.

Punter coughs, not caring where the blood goes. He checks his watch, the numbers glowing digital green in the shadows of the trees. He's not out of time yet, but he can't think of any way to buy more. He decides.

* * *

Once the decision is made, it's nothing to walk into the empty gas station, to push past the waist-high swinging door to get behind the counter. It's nothing to grab the gas station clerk and press the knife through his uniform, into the small of his back. Nothing to ignore the way the clerk squeals as Punter pushes him out from behind the counter.

The clerk says, You don't have to do this.

He says, Anything you want, take it. I don't fucking care, man.

It's nothing to ignore him saying, Please don't hurt me.

It's nothing to ignore the words, to keep pushing the clerk toward the back of the gas station, to the hallway leading behind the coolers. Punter pushes the clerk down to his knees, feels his own feet slipping on the cool tile. He keeps one hand on the knife while the other grips the clerk's shoulder, his fingers digging into the hollows left between muscle and bone.

The clerk says, Why are you doing this?

Punter lets go of the clerk's shoulder and smacks him across the face with the blunt edge of his hand. He chokes the words out.

The girl. I'm here about the girl.

What girl?

Punter smacks him again, and the clerk swallows hard, blood or teeth.

Punter says, You know. You saw her. You told me.

The clerk's lips split, begin to leak. He says, Her? I never did anything to that girl. I swear.

Punter thinks of the clerk's bragging, about how excited he was to be the center of attention. He growls, grabs a fistful of greasy hair, then yanks hard, exposing the clerk's stubbled throat, turning his face sideways until one eye faces Punter's.

The clerk's glasses fall off, clatter to the tile.

The clerk says, Punter.

He says, I know you. Your name is Punter. You come in here all the time.

The clerk's visible eye is wide, terrified with hope, and for one second Punter sees his mother's eyes, sees the girl's, sees his hand closing both their eyelids for the last time.

OSWALD, Punter reads again, then shakes the name clear of his head.

The clerk says, I never hurt her, man. I was just the last person to see her alive.

Punter puts the knife to flesh. It's nothing. We're all the last person to see someone. He snaps his wrist inward, pushes through. That's nothing either. Or, if it is something, it's nothing worse than all the rest.

And then dragging the body into the tiny freezer. And then shoving the body between stacks of hot dogs and soft pretzels. And then trying not to step in the cooling puddles of blood. And then picking up the knife and putting it back in its sheath, tucking it into his waistband again. And then the walk home with a bag of ice in each hand. And then realizing the ice doesn't matter, that it will never be enough. And then the walk turning into a run, his heart pounding and his lungs heaving. And then the feeling he might die. And then the not caring what happens next.

By the time Punter gets back to the garage, the ice is already melting, the girl's face jutting from between the cubes. Her eyelids are covered with frost, cheeks slick with thawing pond water. He reaches in and lifts, her face and breasts and thighs giving to his fingers but her back still frozen to the wrapped venison below. He pulls, trying to ignore the peeling sound her skin makes as it rips away from the paper.

Punter speaks, his voice barely audible. He doesn't have to speak loud for her to hear him. They're so close. Something falls off, but he doesn't look, doesn't need to dissect the girl into parts, into flesh and bone, into brains and blood. He kisses her forehead, her skin scaly like a fish, like a mermaid. He says it again: You're safe now.

He sits down with the girl in his arms and his back to the freezer. He rocks her, feels himself getting wet as she continues to thaw all over him. He shivers, then puts his mouth to hers, breathes deep from the icy blast still frozen in her lungs, lets the air cool the burning in his own throat, the horror of his guts. When he's ready, he picks her up, cradles her close, and carries her into the house. Takes her into the bedroom and lays her down.

He lies beside her, and then, in a loud, clear voice, he speaks. He tries not to cough, tries to ignore the scratchy catch at the back of his throat. He knows what will happen next, but he also knows all this will be over by the time they break down his door, by the time they come in with guns drawn and voices raised. He talks until his voice disappears, until his trapped scream becomes a whisper. He talks until he gets all of it out of him and into her, where none of these people will ever be able to find it.

TEN SCENES FROM A MOVIE CALLED MERCY

It begins with a man walking toward you from the far end of a long hallway, from the end of a courtyard between two symmetrical buildings, from the doorway of a country home and down a packed dirt driveway. You are stationary and he is moving, and though the distances between you are great they are not infinite. Two objects in motion moving down the length of a line cannot remain separated forever. Sooner or later, they must crash into each other and afterward whatever happens next will happen.

A little girl in a sundress pirouettes on a coffee table, her curly red hair encircled in a costume tiara. Her expression is concentration, the grimly pressed lips of a trapeze artist. She spins round and round, and when she stops she is so dizzy she doesn't notice the shadow moving closer, a human form with some sharp darkness clenched in its left hand. The light coming through the window suggests sunrise, sunset, the dusk or the dawn. It suggests choices and borders and the parting of veils between one world and another. When the girl sees the shadow's owner, she begins to scream, a one-note blast as the scene cuts to black.

Forever will not be solved with algebra but with geometry, not with ideas but with things. Even an infinity symbol can be traversed by a single line drawn right. Even the scratchiest record can't skip forever, even the moldiest peach can only decay for so long. Eventually, there is an end to discord, a return to either harmony or silence. After the end credits, there is still the clatter of film against reel, of a machine waiting to be turned off. There is still the need for agency, for someone to help bring everything to a satisfying finale before the lights can come back on.

No one is holding her under the water, not anymore, but still she lies there on the river bottom. She blinks her eyes but does not shut them. The faces of fishes are the last sights she will ever see, their shiny eyes reflective as they float by her. Their lips purse and un-purse wordlessly. She wonders what it would be like to have gills, but not for long. She curls onto her side, turning away from the sunshine slicing uselessly through the surface of the river. Underwater, everything is the same color, and what looked like a riverbed of pebbles from the shore appears here as layers of baby teeth, their cavities worn white again by the flow of water unceasing.

The man again, in a series of jump cuts. The man halfway down the hall. The man halfway across the courtyard. The man halfway down the driveway. The human eye perceives thirty frames a second, so the one frame close-up of his face is too fast to register anywhere conscious. When you immediately start sweating, you will not be able to tell yourself why. Goosebumps spread. These theatres are always so cold.

* * *

A fork, a knife, a spoon on a white linen tablecloth. An apple on a fine china plate. A bite missing, the meat of the apple turned brown in the indent. The voice of a waitress or a mother, asking, Are you done with that? Repeating herself repeatedly: Are you done with that? Are you? Are you done? When you're done with it, you have to throw it away.

Off camera, pray for editing, for the rearrangement of film. The director could take the first scene and throw it away. With a pair of scissors, he could let the second scene tumble to the cutting room floor in a clatter of 8mm frames. Cellulose nitrate is highly flammable, so pray for the fourth scene to be cut short by fire. Pray to keep her safe from the person who wants to hurt her. Take the next scene, throw it away. Resist denouement, resist the solving of mysteries and the revealing of truths, because it is only through these that you may be judged.

Guilt is a loop of footage repeated ad infinitum: He's here. In the hallway and the courtyard and at the end of the driveway, he's here. The man's face is close to your face, and although film captures only sight and sound you know how his breath smells like the aftertaste of white pills manufactured in white factories, distributed by doctors in white coats who promised they would help with the pain, the feeling that was once white but is now a million more complicated colors. The man wears a mask of mirrors. Reflection: a lit cigarette between coarse-stubbled lips, a tiny fire bobbing back and forth. The smoker rocks himself, consoles or controls himself. He has urges. He has needs. They are not necessarily all ones the audience already suspects, but some of them probably are.

Hiding your face from the mirror man will not stop reflection from turning into recognition. You know what you saw, what you did, what you continue to see and do in all too frequent flashbacks. The problem with this film isn't what you see but what you don't. Your flaws are the product of another's too-small imagination, a city limits delineated by bias and slim experience. The director is your only hope, his edits your only chance for revision. He has set himself up to be your savior, if only you'll ask him. If only you'll beg. Beg, we beg of you, beg. For her sake and for your sake.

At last, the forgiveness of new film: A little girl in a sundress pirouettes on a coffee table, her curly red hair encircled in a costume tiara. Her expression is concentration, the grimly pressed lips of a trapeze artist. She spins around and around, and when she stops she is so dizzy she doesn't notice the shadow moving closer, a human form with some sharp darkness clenched in its left hand. The light coming through the window suggests sunrise, sunset, the dusk or the dawn. It suggests choices and borders and the parting of veils between one world and another. The camera lingers long enough that when the girl looks up the shadow is gone. She sits down on the edge of the table, flushed and exhausted. Her legs dangle over the edge, her toes floating just above the floor. She smiles and waves, and when she is ready she stands to repeat her dance all over again. The only thing that captures her is the film, preserving her exactly as she is in that moment, as safe as mere cameras can keep her.

WOLF PARTS

After Red cut her way out of the wolf's belly—after she wiped the gore off her hood and cape, her dress, her tights—she again found herself standing on the path that wound through the forest toward her grandmother's house. Along the way, she met with the wolf, with whom she had palavered the first time and every time since. Afterward, she went to her grandmother's, where she again discovered the wolf devouring the old woman, and where he waited to devour her too, as he had before. Once again she was lost, and once again, she cut herself out of his belly and back onto the stony path. Over and over, she did these things until, desperate to break the cycle, she laid across the stones and, with the knife her mother had given her, gutted herself, quickly, left to right. She cried out in wonder at the bright worlds she found hidden within herself, and with shaky hands she scooped their hot wet flesh into the open air, where with a flick of her wrists she set them each free.

The first time she saw the wolf, she did not run, but let him circle closer and closer, even as his querying yips turned to growls. With one hand, she reached to stroke his fur—full of wretched possibilities, thick and gray and softer than she expected—and with the other she reached into her basket. She dug beneath the jam and pie and paper-wrapped pound of butter for her knife, the only protection her mother had sent with her, as if all it took to keep her safe from the wolf was this tiny silver blade.

At the wolf's suggestion, she left the path to pick some flowers for her grandmother, who was sick and could not care for herself anymore. Tearing each blossom from its roots, she didn't notice the hour growing late, didn't understand the advantage she'd conceded by allowing the wolf to reach the cottage first.

In another version of this story, the flowers cried out warnings of the wolf's trickery, never realizing she could no longer hear their voices. In a previous form, she had lain among their petals and stalks, conversing with them for hours. She had lost this ability when her mother—just days before sending her to her grandmother's—said it was time for her to grow up, to stop acting like a child.

Only his head was that of a wolf. The rest of his body was that of a man, and resembled in all ways that of the only other man she had ever seen without clothes. He had the same hands and arms and legs, the same chest with the same triangle of downy hair that pointed to another thicker thatch of fur below. Even with his wolf's head, the girl was able to recognize his expression, knew that the snarled lips and the exposed canines betrayed the same combination of hunger and apology that she had seen on her father's face years before, when he too had pushed her to the ground and climbed atop her, when he had filled her belly with the same blank stones that the wolf now offered: First gently, then, after she refused, not.

The wolf and Red had always shared the twin paths through the forest, but it wasn't until the girl started to bleed—not a wound, her mother said, but a secret blood nonetheless—that he began to follow her, began to sniff at the hem of her skirts and cape. She asked the wolf what he wanted from her, but he would not use his words, would not form the sounds that might have made clear what he expected her to offer. Instead he nudged her with his muzzle, away from the path of pine needles she had been instructed to walk, and toward the other, thornier path he more often walked alone.

For three days, the grandmother waited in her bed, glued twitching to her sweaty sheets by a fever that choked and burned her, by a hunger that left her furious for foodstuffs, for cakes and butter and tea and wine. For bread that might soak up her fever, if only she was strong enough to get out of the bed to eat.

And then on the third day, a knock, and on the third knock, a voice.

Raise the latch, she cried, before she even fully heard, and certainly before she realized how deep the voice was, and how terribly unlike a little girl's.

* * *

The wolf's breath smelled of chalk, and his paws were covered in flour. It wasn't enough to trick the girl, but she allowed herself to pretend to be fooled. She opened her cloak and invited him in, so that he might do what he came to do.

From inside the wolf's stomach, the grandmother could only hear every third or fourth word her granddaughter spoke, and only slightly more of the wolf's responses. She heard *teeth* and *eyes* and *grandmother.* She heard *better* and *my dear* and *come closer, come closer.*

She heard *to eat you with* and then, with so little time left, she acted, placing her hands against the walls of her wet prison. She pressed and she pushed, stretching the wolf's stomach until it burst, and then she wrapped her hands around the bars of his ribs. When she could not pry her way out, she did not despair. Instead, she opened her mouth into a wide smile, one that—had it happened outside, in the light—would have revealed to the wolf her excellent teeth. She bit down hard, first on lung and heart, then indiscriminately, casting about in a great gnashing, devouring all that she could until the wolf she was inside was also inside her, until she was sure the granddaughter was safe.

The girl dreamed often of the wolf and the grandmother, of the two together, as they were when she found them: The grandmother, with her gasping mouth and her skirts bunched tight in the clenched centers of her fists, and then the wolf, on top of the grandmother with his back arched and his head down, his nose pressed between her legs. In the dream, what captivated her was not the sight of the beast and the woman together, but the sound: the scratch of the wolf's tongue lapping at her grandmother's cleft, at the little red hood atop it. The wolf's tail wagged eagerly, distracting the girl for a second from seeing his engorged penis, the red weight of which she knew was destined for her grandmother's body, if only she did nothing.

She had not done nothing.

With only his voice, the wolf stripped the girl nearly naked, commanding her to remove her shoes and throw them into the fire, then her skirt and bodice, until she wore only her red cape and hood, which she would not remove, no matter how urgently he pleaded.

After she knew the heat of the wolf would keep her warm, she allowed herself to be led outside, where, at his urging, she climbed onto his back. Her body shuddered as his muscles flexed between her legs, as the sharp knuckles of his spine pressed against her. The wolf howled, terrifying and thrilling her at the same time, and then they were off, the wolf bounding faster and faster, carrying her away from all the paths she had known, toward a part of the forest where the brambles were thickest, where without a guide it was possible to get lost forever.

When she would not love him as a boy, he went into the woods and became a wolf, the better to take from her what he wanted. If only he had waited until later, when he was a man and she a woman, their fates might have been different.

* * *

I say *wolf*, but of course there are various kinds of wolves.

Red cried out when she saw the grandmother dressed as a wolf, but calmed herself, breath by breath, until she was ready to listen and learn. After all, it was not the first time the grandmother had changed herself to show Red the shapes she herself might employ one day. When Red was a child, the grandmother had turned into a bird to show her flight, then into a turtle to show her safety. At the time of her first blood, the grandmother had become a boy her own age, and then a woman slightly older, to show her two kinds of physical love that she might one day choose between, and now, as the wolf, the grandmother wanted to show her something else, and if Red did not quite understand what the lesson was, she trusted her grandmother, even though it hurt worse than anything that had come before.

The girl blamed the wolf for leading her off the path, for slowing her while it rushed ahead to devour her grandmother, to paint the lonely cottage with gore. Of course she blamed the wolf. Who would have forgiven her for dooming her grandmother, if she blamed instead the singing birds, the babbling brook, the clustered glamour of a thousand bright forest flowers, ripe for the picking?

She was taken by surprise, despite knowing her sisters had always been jealous of her red chaperon, that dash of color against the dullness of their world. When she awoke, lashed to a tree deep within the forest, she cursed their names loudly and without pause, hoping her father would hear and come to her rescue. After the wolf came instead, her screams turned to stammering, then to pleading. She shut her tear-stung eyes against what she feared was coming, crying out anew as the wolf's hungry breath filled her nostrils. She reopened her eyes only when, instead of the teeth she expected, she felt his tongue rough against her cheeks, licking away her tears. Her fear fell away, was replaced with something else, some other emotion she had not yet experienced, one that was like the affection she felt for her father but darker, more thickly warm and urgent.

Afterward, the wolf chewed through the ropes and freed her from the tree, while she told him about her sisters' betrayal. The wolf howled, and bid her to climb upon his back. His gait was impressive, and his strength even more so when he splintered open the door of their cottage, when he rent and devoured her sisters, as they themselves had hoped he might do to her.

Her father made the wolf's fur into a rug, and laid it in front of the hearth. He said that it would serve as a reminder that his daughter was not to be touched or harmed in any way, that this was the penalty for such a transgression.

Whenever the girl was left alone in the house, she took off the red cape, the clothes beneath it, then she sprawled naked upon the wolf's skin, with her smooth back against his. She touched herself, feeling again the friction of fur, the proximity of some new life she sensed the wolf would have bestowed upon her had they not been caught. When she howled, it was with her mouth against his unhearing ear, her lips close to his stretched and taxidermied jaws, full of the teeth she had just once felt so lovingly against her skin.

On four legs he could easily devour her, could take her in his jaws as fast as he could any deer or rabbit. But on two? On two she was often the one who mastered him.

The wolf tied the girl with silken thread and stashed her in the closet, unsure what to do with her. He was too full from the grandmother to eat, but little girls were rare this deep in the forest. When he heard her thrashing against the closet door, he emitted a low growl meant to frighten her. When the thrashing only intensified, he opened the closet to scare her again, with a flash of teeth or a swipe of paw.

There was no girl inside the closet, only a puddle of thread, cut and discarded.

The wolf did not see the girl again, not for many years. When she returned, grown lovely and stubborn and brave, he himself had declined, aged and weak. He was not sorry for what he'd done—he was a wolf, after all—but still he cried out for mercy. The girl acted as if she couldn't hear him, scowling as she twisted her own ropes around his body, binding him still before setting to work on him in the same fashion he'd once intended for her—with sharp objects meant to cut, meant to tear, meant to render meat separate from bone.

* * *

With blade and trap, with fire and water, with drowning and crushing and boiling and slashing and cutting and stabbing: These are just some of the ways she killed them, one after the other.

After the incident, Red became a great enemy of the wolves, vowing that never again would she wait for one of their kind to molest her upon the path. She took to the woods in her hooded cape, knowing the wolves would see her coming, but also that this warning would not be enough to save them. She tanned and sewed and dyed each of their hides, then gave away the fur-trimmed cloaks to the women of her village until the whole of the woods was filled with red hoods and red capes, each of them concealing a girl or a woman, a knife or an axe.

Given the opportunity, he chose once more to be a man instead of a wolf, and by doing so he gained certain abilities, lost others entirely. His man's face and courtier's clothes made it easier for him to lure his prey—not the deer and elk he had recently hunted, but the other, comelier prey he had long desired—and certainly he believed he had made the right choice, even if he no longer smelled as acutely, could no longer hear a doe approaching from miles away. This is how he failed to sense the women following him out of the village and into the woods, how he didn't notice until it was too late that each of them carried her own small knife, her own sharp stone. When they pinned him down in the thistles beside the path, he howled as each of them made a cut in a place of their choosing, then again, as their tiny fingers shoved their stones through the openings they had made.

As commanded, she climbed into the bed naked, speaking in soft, mock-innocent syllables, pretending not to notice that the figure in the nightgown was not her grandmother, so that the great, hairy wolf would feel safe to reveal his true intentions. She waited, polite and acquiescent, and as soon as the wolf forced himself inside her, she sprung her trap, showing him that she too knew what it meant to consume someone whole.

An axe is a knife is a pair of sewing scissors: Tools as weapons, weapons as tools. Ways to cut yourself out from inside a wolf or, in other circumstances, to cut your way back in.

Red and her grandmother had seen this trick before, and so could not be taken by surprise. Red refused to leave the path, the grandmother declined to open the door, and when they each questioned the wolf through the bolted wood, they already knew the cheap answers he would offer. The only one surprised was the wolf, who knew not where these women had gotten their knives, nor where they had learned the sharp skill with which they wielded them.

Every winter, the villagers sent one of their own girls into the forest as tribute. Although the wolf promised to return each girl by spring, it had been years since any had made their way home, as they once had. Even back then, they returned damaged, scarred, bereft, hardly the girls they had been before their time with the wolf. With few options remaining, the villagers had no choice but to send Red in place of the too-lovely girl they had previously chosen. At twelve, Red was almost too old for the wolf's tastes, but the villagers were sure that her radiant innocence would win him over, would please the ravener they all feared so much.

Before sending her down the path, they gave her a red riding hood, the better to see her when she emerged from the forest, and they gave her a knife, sharp as the wolf's own teeth, the better to saw her way from his belly when the time came.

For months the villagers fretted and worried. Then, when the sun was highest on the first day of spring, they saw Red appear at the tree line, her face grim and her forearm—still clutching the knife—covered in slick gore. In her other hand she held the hand of a child, and that child held another and then another and then another.

The villagers rejoiced, and praised Red above all others, but she did not join them in celebration. No matter how they pleaded for her company, she remained apart, her face a slab of pale skin and blank teeth. By the time she departed the following winter, the villagers were glad to see her go. Although they made great shows of protestation in front of each other, they knew she was changed by what she had done, and while they would not say so aloud, each secretly feared the sight of her hood, of the knife she still carried whole seasons after she had last needed it.

* * *

In another telling, Red never returned, and in the following years there appeared more and more wolves in the woods around the forest, until the villagers felt afraid to walk the path leading to the city. Each of these new pups had thick red fur, and when they howled in unison at the moon, it was in one voice, less like that of a wolf and more like a woman screaming, like a girl who, if the rumors in the city were true, the villagers had knowingly sent to be raped and tortured and, after she gave birth, torn limb from pale-fleshed limb.

Or maybe Red returned not with a line of small girls, but with the wolf himself in tow, a rope turned cruel around his neck and her knife wet with his protests. In this version, it wasn't until she reached the village center that she slit the wolf from throat to tail. Too late, she retrieved each and every child from the wolf's stomach, each of them bruised and bloodied and without breath. In anger, the villagers filled the wolf's belly with stones while Red held close his howling head, counting for him the many names of these dead children, the many pounds of shale and limestone it would take to buy their penance.

If the wolf had always been the wolf, and the grandmother always the grandmother, why did Red so often struggle to tell them apart? Perhaps it was because, after pulling her knife from the wolf's flesh, she frequently found wet scraps of bloodied nightgown stuck to the blade, or else how, while kissing her grandmother's pursed lips, she so often tasted raw meat rotting from between the older woman's teeth.

* * *

The wolf had expected the girl to protest, but she continued eating the flesh and drinking the blood that he served her, until her clothes were wet and matted, until her mouth was stained the color of her cape. Their goblets overflowed, then tipped and dripped onto the cottage floor. The grandmother was a bigger woman out of her skin than she had seemed in it, so the wolf, tired from his gluttony, yawned once, twice, a third time. He could not stop yawning. With his head thrown back and his engorged throat exposed, he realized too late that the girl was crawling across the table, her face filthy with the wet horror of their meal. Clenching her fork and knife in her tiny fists, she searched the empty platters, and when she found nothing else to eat, she clambered quickly toward the yawning wolf, hungry for more.

The girl was surprised when she slid her hand between the wolf's muscular, furred legs, to find that he was a *she*, something she had never considered, not even when she saw her dressed in her grandmother's clothes, so calm and perfect, reclining gorgeous against those many plush pillows.

He was a pup, a boy, a wolf, a man, a wolfman, a woodsman. He was all of these, but never more than one at a time. He changed with the moon, and then, later, according to his own whim. When he came to her at night, it was always as a wolf, a shape she grew to love, even though it had cost her everything she had once known. Even after the deaths of her mother and grandmother, she preferred the wolf to the man, to that shape that had failed to protect her time and time again, without ever understanding that her choice was no choice at all.

The wolf was trapped as soon as he dressed himself in the grandmother's clothes. The bonnet grew tighter and tighter, its taut ribbons cutting into his throat and choking his jaw, while the nightgown's sleeves immobilized his forepaws, made useless his claws. When he tried to take a deep breath to give air to a howl, he found only whimpers left within his lungs, all the air crushed out of him by the constricting nightclothes.

Several tortured hours passed before the women came for him, and by the time they arrived, the wolf was past pitiful. Weaker women might have felt mercy temper their vengeance, but not the grandmother, and certainly not her daughter's daughter, whose flat smile betrayed a heart as hard and heavy as an unskippable stone. With their saws and their hatchets and their sharp knowledge of knives, they fed the wolf piece by screaming piece to their fire, and when they were finished with him, they buried the slim remains— teeth and eyes and spleen and genitals—beneath a pile of rocks so unremarkable that even they could never quite remember where in the wide woods it was.

After the mother and grandmother both passed away, the wolf took their places, so that the girl he secretly adored would not have to go without. The wolf raced back and forth between their two houses, switching between the mother's apron and the grandmother's gown, raising his voice as high as it would go. For her part, the girl pretended not to notice, but it was hard, and sooner or later she knew she would slip, or else he would, and then they would have to act like girls and wolves were supposed to act, with howling and screaming and the gnashing of teeth and knives, until they were each alone once again.

The woodsman and the wolf had been friends once, and what happened between them in the grandmother's cottage a mere misunderstanding. Seeing the wolf there in his mother's clothing, the woodsman mistook him for the woman he had come to kill. It wasn't until after his axe blade slowed—when he was able to see past his blinding matricide to the fur that covered the floor—that he realized his mistake, and was ashamed.

The grandmother hungered, consumed with her sickness, and in her crazed state she tore the young girl's limbs from her body with fever-strong twists, devouring each one over the course of several screaming days. When the wolf came to visit, he saw what she had done, and in his mercy he devoured the grandmother too, so that she would not have to live with the sin, so that others would not know what this once great woman had become.

The wolf grew skilled at counterfeiting the girl's voice. He gained entry into many of her haunts in this way, murdering her family and friends as he went, until his belly dragged on the ground as an animal, hung over his belt as a man. Sometimes, when she joined him in their bed, she laid her cheek upon the fur of his belly and listened to the grumbling from within, to the voices of all her kith and kin he had devoured on his way to loving her. They cried out for her to save them, but she had her wolf, and he was all she needed.

Come get into bed with me, said the wolf, said the grandmother, said the woodsman, said the girl. Each of them made their voice exactly what another wanted to hear, using the perfect enunciation and tone designed to lure them as completely as possible, and to each other they were lost.

Satiated, the wolf slumbered. His belly rose and fell with each breath, each drunken snore. Inside his swollen stomach he'd trapped little girls and mothers and grandmothers, woodsmen by the dozens. All around them were trees and deer and rabbits and birds and flowers, even the remains of a river, drunk greedily a week or a month before. The wolf himself couldn't remember, had been nearly mad with hunger and thirst, and in his madness had consumed all that he could. The wolf slept on, and when he awoke he was surrounded by the shattered ruins of a cottage, and beyond that a vast field of furrowed, rent dirt. He could no longer feel all those he'd swallowed kicking at his stomach, trying to force their way back out. Satisfied, the wolf grinned—a wolf's grin, all teeth—and then he tried to rise, only to find that his feast had turned hard and heavy as stone. No matter how he struggled, he could not stand, nor crawl against the distended weight of his belly, and soon there was nothing left within the reach of his desperate jaws.

If I told you the wolf deserved this lonely end, that his slow, struggling starvation was justified, then that would be one kind of tale. But he was not a moral wolf, and this was never about to become a moral story, no matter how it ended.

So little yet endured! Just the girl, with her red hood, her red cape, her red-slicked knife, with which she was still slashing her own story to pieces, still discovering new and radiant shapes of pain and pleasure, until all that remained was the last dirge of the wolf, howling with hungered frustration, joined by the cries of her own failing voice, each matching the other's song note for bloody note.

MANTODEA

From across the bar, I couldn't stop staring at her, at that breathtaking mouth of hers. Obviously as orally obsessed as I was, she filled that laughing cavity with whatever was close at hand: lime wedges, olives, tiny black straws she chewed between cigarettes. Gallons of vodka or gin, I couldn't see which. She cracked ice cubes between strong white teeth, the sound audible even above the jukebox and the clatter and clack of pool balls coming together, spiraling apart. I wanted to stick my fist in there, to get her bright red lipstick all over my watchband.

Getting up from my table in the corner, I steadied myself on chair backs and unoffered shoulders. The floor was the sticky history of a thousand spilled nights, and other couples danced between the pool tables and the bathrooms, their shoes making flypaper two-steps to the country-western songs spilling from the jukebox. I weaved between them until I reached the bar, where I took the stool beside the woman.

I lit a cigarette, signaled the bartender for another whiskey with a raised pair of fingers. From up close, the woman was all mouth, the rest of her thin, too thin, hungry and lean like cancer. I wondered about the nutritional value of her life, of everything that passed through the furious red smear of her lips. I imagined both our mouths working furiously on each other, kissing with jaws unhinged as snakes.

I turned toward her, lifted my glass. Tried to remember how to smile without opening my mouth. Felt I probably wasn't doing it exactly right.

Her own mouth said, Whatever it is you're thinking of saying, it's probably the wrong thing.

I waited before I responded. Waited until the urge passed to tell her about my old life, about all that I swallowed in the months before the hospital. I wanted to tell her though. Wanted to tell her about the coins and thumbtacks and staples. The handfuls of dirt and crushed light bulbs.

I wanted to tell her that like a lot of poisons you might eat, you have to swallow a lot more drain cleaner than you'd expect, if you're trying to kill yourself. At least, the stuff hadn't worked on me, not as I'd once hoped it would.

What it had done was clear me out, get rid of all kinds of things that had once been stuck inside of me. That had backed me up.

What it had done was take away my lower intestine, give me a short throw of a colon that couldn't handle spicy food or even most solids. No citrus or tomatoes. No milk or milk products.

This new body, it wasn't supposed to be exposed to alcohol, but giving up the booze was never really an option.

What I said to her instead was, I like watching you eat, drink.

I want to buy you a meal.

A meal with courses. Appetizer. Soup. Salad. Fish. Meat. Miniature loaves of bread with mounded pats of butter.

I said, I want to watch you eat desserts that you have to chew and chew. Taffy. Caramels. I want to give you hard candies to suck thin and crush between your molars.

I said, I'd lick all the sticky sugar off your teeth for hours, if you wanted me to.

Her mouth laughed, said, The only meals I eat I find at the bottom of cocktail glasses.

She fished her olive from under her ice cubes and popped it into her mouth, then licked clear liquor off her dripping fingers. I watched a single drop spill down the back of her hand, trace the blue ridge of a vein from knuckle to wrist. I laughed too, but with a hand over my mouth, hiding the teeth destroyed by chewing steel, the gums peeled black by the Drano. She reached over and pulled my hand down, saying, When I was a little girl, I thought mastication and masturbation were exactly the same word.

She had a disorienting smile, and for a moment I didn't know who was aggressing who. She laughed again, slipped off the barstool with a swish of skirt. Drained her glass.

Her mouth said, It's not love at first sight, but it is something, isn't it?

She walked away, past the pool tables and the dancing couples, their temporary lusts. I watched as she pushed through the swing of the bathroom door. I stubbed out my cigarette, finished my drink, then walked toward the bathroom myself, my guts burning and my throat scratched with smoke, my brain brave and dumb as a lizard's. I put my hand on the cool metal panel of the bathroom door. I pushed.

The bathroom was two stalls and a single sink beneath an empty frame that once held a mirror presumably busted by some drunken stumble. She was inside the near stall, the smaller one. There was less room to move than there would have been in the handicapped stall, but there was enough.

The door wouldn't lock, but I didn't care. Her back was to me, that glorious mouth seen only briefly when she looked over her shoulder, the wet slash of her lips framed by the toss of her chopped blond hair. I wanted her to turn around, but I thought she was teasing me, even though she wanted what I wanted or something close enough to count. She didn't look back again, just put her hands against the slick tile wall, planted her feet on each side of the toilet. Waited for me. When I got close, the nape of her neck smelled like bad habits, tasted worse. I didn't care. I wasn't there to feel nice. Neither of us were. She flinched slightly at the sound of my belt buckle striking the porcelain toilet seat, then asked me my name. I whispered a fake one, then told her the truth when she asked me to repeat myself, knowing she'd assume it was a lie.

Right before I finished, I felt her back arch toward me, felt her hands reaching for my face, pulling it close to hers. Her mouth opened, taking in my cheeks then my nose then my right eye, the whole side of my mouth. I felt her teeth tugging at the scratchy pouch between my ear and my jaw line, wanted her to keep going, to keep devouring me until I was gone.

I'd once thought I wanted to eat something that could end me, but now I knew I really wanted something else, something approximately the opposite. Something this woman could give me.

Later, after it was over, I realized she'd wanted the same thing, that I'd failed her by not tearing her to pieces, by not taking her inside me one bite at a time.

Too focused on myself, what I thought instead—right before I pulled out of her, before she pushed me against the stall divider with her tiny wrists full of their fragile bird bones, and definitely before she slipped past me without giving me the last kiss I so desperately wanted—what I thought then was, This one time will never be enough.

Still misunderstanding everything, what I said was, I'm going to need to see you again.

Her mouth laughed as she exited the bathroom, the sound so loud my ears were already ringing by the time I got my pants up. I raced after her, out of the bar and into the cold parking lot, where I lost her to the night's thick blanket of confusion, its sharp starlight and fuzzed out streetlamps.

I waited for the sound to stop, and eventually it did. Nothing she'd done would turn out to be permanent. Her smell would be gone by morning, and the teeth marks on my face would take less than a week to scab over and then, to my terror, heal completely.

For the first time in months, I went home to my apartment and emptied the kitchen junk drawer onto the dining table. I picked up the tiny nails and paper clips and stubs of pencils and erasers and whatever else I could find and then I jammed them into my system. I considered pouring myself a drink, then stopped and took a long hot swallow from the bottle. I smashed the unnecessary tumbler on the corner of the counter, watched as the cheap glass shattered everywhere. Stepping carefully so as not to cut my bare feet, I picked up the most wicked shard I could find. I held it in my hand, then set it in my mouth, rested it on my tongue. I swallowed hard, and when I didn't die I went back for more.

THE LEFTOVER

What happened with Allison and Jeff was what was happening all the time, to other people Allison knew and, she presumed, to lots of people she didn't know. They had met, dated until it seemed like they should probably move in together, and then lived together until it seemed they should stop. In between, they talked about getting married, about buying a house, about having a family, but they didn't do any of those things. Now they were broken up, and there had been no fighting, no harsh words, just the knowledge that something had ended.

He was gone and she was still here.

That is what she has decided she will say to people when they ask her how she's feeling and if she's all right.

She will say, I am still here. She will say it like it means something all by itself, like quitting or being quit on is the easiest thing in the world.

When Allison wakes up the morning after the breakup, she sits up in bed and listens. She'd dreamed Jeff was there, but of course he isn't. She goes into the bathroom to brush her teeth and take a shower, where the mirror reveals she's wearing one of Jeff's old shirts he must have left behind. She hates missing him so obviously, but tells herself that she put it on after two bottles of red wine and so isn't really responsible for the decision.

As she gets out of the shower and starts toweling off, she hears the television blaring in the living room. She knows she didn't leave it on, as she barely watches it. She wraps her towel around herself, too wet to be running around the apartment, but she doesn't care. Her head's pounding as she charges through the bedroom and into the living room to confront Jeff and tell him to get the hell out and then she screams, because the person on the couch is not Jeff.

By the time she's finished, Allison has seen enough that she doesn't have to ask who this person is.

What she has to ask is how this person is. Not on a friendly level, but an existential one.

The intruder isn't Jeff, but improbably, he is Jeff, too. A smaller version of Jeff, maybe four or five feet tall. Smaller, but not younger, although this person does remind her of her Jeff a few years ago. He's got the goatee she made Jeff shave off and he's smoking a cigarette clenched nonchalantly between two thin fingers, even though Allison made her Jeff quit the same time she did.

This miniature imposter, he waves at her with a perfect copy of Jeff's overly enthusiastic wave.

Allison asks, Who are you? How did you get in here?

The tiny man shrugs. He's wearing a t-shirt that Jeff used to wear when they first started dating. Jeff had gotten it from a track meet when he was a runner in high school, and by the time they met it was threadbare and faded. She'd made him throw it out and yet here it was, looking the same as it had that day.

She asks, Can't you talk?

He shakes his head, turns back to the television. Allison doesn't know what to do, so she walks around to the front of the couch and sits beside him. He looks the way old photographs do: recognizable but not too, like someone she used to know but not the person she's just broken up with.

Little Jeff—she doesn't know what else to call him—he looks up at her with a smile as he takes another puff from his cigarette. It's been over a year since she's smelled smoke in the apartment, and the smell makes her both irritated and nostalgic. She opens her mouth, wanting to ask for a cigarette, then represses the urge, as she always does. It's one thing Allison is proud of: When she quits something, she stays quit.

It's a Sunday and Allison doesn't have to work, so she takes Little Jeff to the movies. It's where she and Jeff went on their first date, one of the few places where she can be reasonably sure she won't have to talk for at least two hours. They watch a comedy that Allison swears she's seen before, even though the ticket price assures her it's a new release. During the beginning of the movie, Little Jeff sits beside her, his eyes fixed on the screen and his hand making a perpetual motion from the popcorn bucket to his mouth and back again. He chomps loudly, irritating her, but before she can say anything he finishes eating, then reaches over and holds her hand, his small fingers cool and comfortable and reassuring in hers.

After the movie, Allison drives them to the chain restaurant closest to the theater. This is where she and Jeff went after their first movie together. She sits across from Little Jeff without saying anything, both of them smiling a bit too much while she tries not to embarrass herself by making a mess of her food. By the time Allison gets home, she's sure this has been the best day she's had in months. All weirdness aside, she's happy, and that's something.

In the apartment, Little Jeff strips to his underwear and climbs into bed, a development Allison isn't comfortable with. She doesn't know what to say, so she goes to sleep on the couch. She thinks again about her first date with Jeff, how she wanted to sleep with him but didn't want him to think badly about her. She wonders what Jeff thought that night. She wonders what Little Jeff is thinking right now.

The next day at work, Allison is supposed to be proofreading the newest edition of a calculus textbook, but there's no way she can concentrate. What she does instead is search the internet: *Doppelganger. Clone. Homunculus.* She follows the links from one site to the next, trying to find a description that at least approximates the person in her living room.

What she finds is nothing very useful.

She opens a new document and types CHARACTERISTICS OF LITTLE JEFF then makes a list: Smoker. Doesn't like health food. Chews with his mouth open. Watches too much television. Doesn't put his clothes in the hamper.

It doesn't take her long to recognize the pattern, to see that what Little Jeff is made of is all that she made her first Jeff quit or change or give up. She's lost her boyfriend and gained all the things she hated about him, and yet she wishes she could be home instead of at work. She thinks about calling Jeff but she knows she'll sound crazy, so she calls her apartment instead.

Little Jeff answers on the third ring but doesn't speak. Allison says, I just called to make sure you're okay.

Allison doesn't know what to say next, what she expected to happen. She holds the phone to her ear a little longer, listening to Little Jeff breathe, and then she says goodbye and hangs up the phone. She decides that on the way home she'll pick up a bucket of fried chicken and some mashed potatoes. Once upon a time, it was Jeff's favorite food.

Allison once again gets used to dirty clothes on the floor, socks under the coffee table, skid-marked underwear kicked beside the tub. After a week, she's used to the fact that even though she works all day she's still going to have to do the dishes when she comes home. Ditto for cooking dinner, for doing laundry, for making sure the rent gets paid on time.

The next cable bill that comes, she's furious at the seven dollars and ninety-nine cents she's been billed for a porno. She charges into the living room with the bill clenched in her hand, but then she remembers how she freaked out when Jeff did the same thing, thinking he wouldn't get caught, and how her yelling didn't do either of them any good.

During this same time period, she comes to understand that it's not only the bad habits Jeff quit that make up Little Jeff. There are also qualities that Allison forgot she even missed, because they've been gone so long or because they disappeared from her and Jeff's relationship without announcing their departure. She notices the long absence of these traits only when they reemerge: Little Jeff writes poems on the backs of take out receipts and on yellow sticky notes, just like Jeff used to do. She finds them in odd places, as if Little Jeff doesn't understand that it might be more romantic to put them on her side of the bed or on her nightstand. She finds a haiku—*freezer door left open / letting out the stark cold air / I am apology*—taped to a box of her tampons, then free verse tucked into the toes of her galoshes. The poems aren't good exactly, but she takes them from their hiding places and puts them in the scrapbook where she kept Jeff's poems, then, unsure if she should treat them as two separate authors, she removes them and starts a new collection. These new poems are written by someone who is like Jeff but is not him, unless she counts the leavings of a body as part of a person. Unless she counts the dead skin cells ground into her carpet or the sweat soaked permanently into the mattress, the one lone hair stuck in the drain of their shower because she is too lazy to dislodge it. She could count these things as Jeff but doesn't, and if these things are not Jeff, then neither is this other person.

The first time she has sex with Little Jeff is the best sex she's had in a year. What Little Jeff knows about her is what Jeff used to know, back when he cared more about her happiness than his own. Afterward, with Little Jeff curled against her longer body, she recognizes this is unfair, but she thinks it again anyway. She has always wondered why her friends are constantly falling into bed with their ex-boyfriends and now she understands. It is good to be known, to have your likes and dislikes already clear before the act even begins.

* * *

Three months after Jeff moves out, Allison is still learning to take the good with the bad, to put up with the boogers stuck to her furniture if it means she gets poems tucked in her purse. She hates that Little Jeff smokes so much, but she doesn't ask him to quit. She doesn't ask him to change anything, at first because she doesn't want to drive him away and then later because she is afraid of what will happen to whatever he quits.

Whatever she and Little Jeff have, it may end one day, and then what? What if another, smaller version comes to live with her?

This time, she'll let her man do whatever he wants, be whoever he needs to be, and she'll decide whether to stay or go based on who he is, not who she wants him to be.

Together, they go to other places that Jeff and Allison went when they were new. They go to an art museum that Allison has wanted to see forever, and they go to a movie that Little Jeff picks out of the paper, some remake of an eighties cartoon that Allison never watched and still doesn't like. They go to the botanical gardens, a place people only go when they start dating or when they get married or when they are a thousand years old. Allison is glad that Little Jeff has so much facial hair or else she would have to worry that people would think she was letting her kid smoke. As it is, they hold hands and kiss and she learns to stop caring what other people think they see. She has often made choices because someone else told her she should, because she read about a new diet in a magazine or because her friends were all doing the same. Little Jeff is everything she took from Jeff by doing this, and it's enough for her to see she doesn't want to be that way ever again.

One day, Allison comes home from work with an armload of groceries, thrilled at the truly decadent meal she's making for the two of them for dinner. Nowhere in her bags is any organic fruit or wheatgrass or any labels with the words *high-fiber* on them. Instead, she's cooking footlong coney dogs, with chili out of a can and onions out of a plastic bag. She's frying French fries and making root beer floats. She knows eating this is going to make her sick, but she also knows it's going to make Little Jeff happy.

She sits her groceries down on the counter and calls for him but there's no answer. It takes her a minute to realize that the television is dark, that it isn't tuned to sports news or the endless reruns of crime procedural shows that always seem to be on. Walking through the apartment, she notices other things: There are no clothes on the floor of the bathroom, no wads of tissue crumpled along Little Jeff's side of the bed.

She's nearly in a panic trying to find him, but eventually she does. He's outside on the apartment's small balcony, somewhere she's never seen him go before. There isn't any furniture out there, so he's sitting on the concrete.

It takes her a minute to realize he's crying. In the years she was with the real Jeff, she never saw him cry, and so Allison doesn't know what to do. She reaches in her purse and offers Little Jeff a cigarette from the pack she purchased herself a few days ago, after convincing herself that she'd been quit long enough that it was okay to have just one. Little Jeff shakes his head, his eyes brimming, and it's only then that Allison realizes what seemed different about the apartment. It hadn't smelled like smoke when she came in.

Little Jeff's quit smoking.

She drops her purse and scoops him up in her arms, and as he curls against her she can feel he's lost weight, and although it takes a little longer to be sure, she sees he's lost height too, that he is even smaller than he was before. Even his facial hair is thinning, fading from a full goatee to a tiny triangle of soul patch.

Allison is furious, but not at Little Jeff, who she keeps rocking and reassuring that everything will be okay, even though she's sure that it won't be, that if she doesn't do something then he'll be gone soon.

She needs to call Jeff. Needs to tell him not to stop quitting everything she made him quit, because she's sure that's what's happened.

She wants a cigarette, craves it intensely, but she fights the urge. It's taken her months, but she's finally realizing that Little Jeff might not be the only thing leftover from the breakup.

Little Jeff falls asleep alone that night, pushed all the way over on his side of the bed, as if he recognizes that his diminishing size has changed the physical dynamic between them. He's child-like in a way he wasn't only a day before, and the idea of him as a lover is past. Allison lies awake, staring at him and wondering what her own counterpart might look like. She tries to remember all she quit while Jeff and she dated. Smoking is a given, but other things are vaguer. Which of Allison's haircuts would her leftover sport? She flips through the mental images she has of herself, eventually settling on the long perm she'd had when they started dating. Jeff had liked it, but had encouraged her to try something new, something more contemporary.

What else? Allison thinks about her job at the textbook publisher, about how she hates it but has never looked for anything else. She thinks about all the careers she wanted instead, and wonders if they count as things that she quit or if they were never what she actually was. She had wanted to be a gymnast as a little girl, and then an astronaut. She had played the flute in junior high, but gave it up in high school to try to date a different class of boy than what she found in the band. She owns a bike she never uses. Ditto rollerblades. Ditto yoga videos.

This Little Allison, she might wear hideous blue eyeliner or have terribly outdated tastes in clothing, but Allison doesn't really think that's all of it.

Most of what Allison has quit are good things, things that might have made her happier than she is. She doesn't have bad habits, just bad follow-through.

Little Jeff is snoring quietly, his tiny hands folded over his belly. She wonders if she is supposed to stop Jeff from starting up all his old bad habits, or if she is supposed to encourage him until this other vanishes completely.

Watching Little Jeff sleep, she wonders if he's dreaming. If he dreams. She wonders if it hurt when he shrank, or if it was just something that happened. She wishes he could talk so he could tell her what he wanted her to do.

She gets out of bed and reaches for her phone. Dials Jeff's cell. It rings and rings and then, right before the voicemail should click on, he answers, his voice groggy with sleep.

He says, Hello? Allison?

She hangs up by slamming the clamshell shut, then turns the phone off so he can't call her back. She sits in the dark with the phone clenched between her hands until she's sure of what she wants to do, and then she gets up and does it. Gets dressed. Puts her shoes on. Goes downstairs to the parking lot and moves her car close to the front of the building, then goes back upstairs with the engine running.

Quietly, Allison wraps the sleeping boy in his blanket and carries him down to the car. He's so small. She wishes she had a car seat for him but she doesn't. She'll have to be careful. He stirs when she buckles him in but doesn't wake up, only sticks his thumb in his mouth and sucks hard. She gets in the driver's seat and just drives.

At Jeff's new place, Allison peeks in the bedroom window, her toes digging into the soft dirt around his bushes. It takes a minute for her eyes to adjust, but thankfully Jeff's sleeping with his television on, something she never would have let him do.

Not that she cares. She doesn't, for real this time, and anyway she's not there to see Jeff, or at least not just Jeff. She's there to see if she's there too.

And she is.

There, like a doll tucked into Jeff's arms, is a tiny version of her, complete with the long hair Allison predicted. On the nightstand are the bulky red glasses she got rid of in college, folded neatly beside a glass of water. It's all she can see from the bushes, but it's enough.

The only other thing she sees—the very last detail before she turns away from the window—is how happy they both look. How contented. How like a father and a daughter.

She wants to look like that too. Wants to look like that with them. Wants to look like a family, with him and him and her.

She wants to stop quitting and then unquitting. She wants to stop hurting people by doing one or the other. She wants to stick with something and make it work this time, no matter what.

Allison doesn't know what will happen when Jeff meets Little Jeff, or when she meets Little Allison, but that doesn't matter. She's tired of all the warnings, all the shows and magazines and well-intentioned friends telling her it's too risky to do this thing or that thing. All the voices telling her she can't do what she wants.

She walks back to her car and opens the passenger door, then crouches down and carefully unbuckles the sleeping boy. Little Jeff slings his arms around her neck like the toddler he's becoming, and she lifts him with an arm tucked under his hips. Even in the dim glow of the dome light she can see how young he looks. His facial hair is completely gone, and he's even a little pudgy, a little fat in the cheeks. Allison kisses him on his forehead, then carries him up the walk toward Jeff's front door. She doesn't know what any of this is or what it might mean, but she's willing to try anyway, to trust that together they can make it work.

She reaches for the doorbell. She rings it. She thinks of what to say, of the dozens of ways she might say what she needs to. She settles on one, and when the door opens she says it as fast as she can, trying to make a million new promises all at once.

A CERTAIN NUMBER OF BEDROOMS, A CERTAIN NUMBER OF BATHS

The boy carries the blueprint catalogs everywhere he goes. At school, he keeps them in his backpack, only occasionally looking inside to spy their colorful covers, comforted simply by their presence, their proximity. It is different at home. After school, he locks himself in the empty house and sits at the kitchen table, where he fans the catalogs out in front of him as he eats his snack. He compares the artist's renditions on the left page with the floor plans on the right, then moves to the living room floor, where he watches television and turns the thin catalog pages. He mutes his cartoons so he can hear himself enunciating the names of the homes he hopes his father will build.

Ranches: Crestwood, Echo Hills, Nova.

Split Levels: Timber Ridge, Elk Ridge.

The Capes: Cod, Vincent, and Chelsey.

Two-story houses, like the one they live in, in ascending order by size: Walden, Westgate, Somerset, Carbondale.

The boy has not been reading long and wants to be sure that when the time comes he can spell the new house's name, that he can say it. He pronounces slowly, then more confidently. He wants the new home to be built from the ground up, so it will not have anyone else's history attached to it, so that he knows for sure that no one will have died in the garage. He often wonders if they would be better off without a garage at all.

Only after his father's obsession with the catalogs passed did the boy take them to his own room. He thought he'd get in trouble for claiming them but never did, not even later when he started sneaking them to school in his backpack. The boy is years away from the time he steals his first porno magazine from beneath his father's mattress, but when he does he will remember the catalogs, remember the feel of their crinkly, hand-worn pages. Once again, he will find himself too young to understand what he's looking at or why he wants it, the magazines reminding him only obliquely of this time in his life, when so much hope is invested in so little paper.

At dinner, the boy tells his father about the houses he likes best this week, about how he is having trouble deciding between the Crestwood and the Cape Cod. The father glances at the pages as the boy presents them. A month ago he smiled at the boy's enthusiasm, even joined in with comments of his own, but now he is less demonstrative with his opinions.

Dinner: A meal consisting of brand-name hot dogs and macaroni and cheese. The father is not frugal with his shopping as the mother was. He buys what he recognizes, assured by television that he is making a good choice.

The boy has been in so few other houses that actually picturing the interior of any other home means simply reconfiguring the rooms of their own house into his conception of the new one. The floor plans he likes best are ones he can most easily shoehorn his own into, using the homes of his grandmother and of the neighbor boy his mother once forced him to play with to fill in the bigger houses. The father does not say much in return, but the boy has become used to this. To make up for his father's reticence, the boy talks more and more, more than he is comfortable with, not because he wants to but because he does not like the silence at the table, the reminder that there is something missing, that without her they are alone even when they are with each other.

Suicide: Car running, windows closed, parked in the garage. No one would ever drive it again and two months after her death it would be sold at a loss. The boy was not supposed to find her. She did not know that school had become a half day, that everyone had been sent home early because of the impending snowfall. The note taped to the outside of the driver's window was addressed to his father, not to him. The boy could barely read then, but decided to try anyway. He pulled the note off the window, leaving the scotch tape behind.

Mother: Hidden underneath. Pressed against the window with her mouth open, the steam from her breath slowly disappearing from the cloudy glass. The last time he saw her.

9-1-1: The boy had learned the number in school, but he had not been taught that it was not failsafe, that it did not save everyone. For months he thought about raising his hand and telling his teacher about her error, but they had moved on from health and safety and would not speak of it again.

Extolling the virtues of the houses to the father, the boy lists the numbers of bedrooms and bathrooms. He wonders what half a bathroom is but does not ask. He explains that all the houses from American Homes have R-19 insulation, which he has been assured by the catalog is the very best kind. He shows his father the cross section of a wall and repeats from memory the phrase *oriented strand board*. The boy pronounces many of the words wrong. He does not realize that learning words by sounding them out alone has left him with false pronunciations, sounds that as an adult he will be constantly corrected for. No matter how hard he tries to hide it, he will not speak the same language others speak.

Father: Quiet. Sluggish. Often watches the news from his easy chair with his eyes closed. A tumbler of melting, browning ice dangles from his fingertips at all times. Has apparently forgotten how to play catch or even how to get to the park.

Father (previous): Fun. Loud. Told jokes the mother disapproved of but that the boy loved. Often rustled the boy's hair, which the boy pretended to hate but secretly didn't. Missing in action.

Father (future): Defined by the loss of his partner in a way he was never defined by her presence.

* * *

The boy reads the catalogs in the evening while his father naps in his recliner. His father rarely makes it to the bedroom anymore and so sometimes the boy sleeps on the couch to be near him. More often he goes to his own room, where he reads the catalogs until he is too tired to keep his eyes open. Each night, before he sleeps, he chooses the home he thinks they need, his decisions changing quickly, like moods or Michigan weather. Sometimes he falls asleep with the light on, and those nights are the ones he stays in his bed.

On other nights, the boy wakes up shaking, then walks into the living room where his father sleeps. Standing beside the recliner, the boy tries to will his father to wake up before starting to shake him. Neither tactic works. The father snores on, even when the boy begins at last to talk, begins to insist that his father talk back, that he take them away from this home which is no longer any such thing.

Eventually his teacher notices the black rings below his eyes and keeps him inside at recess. She asks him if there's anything he wants to talk about, if maybe something is happening at home. He knows she knows, but if she will not say so, then neither will he. The boy does not show her the catalogs, hides their meaning from anyone who might accidentally see and ask. Curiosity is not the same as caring.

The new house will end up being an apartment, a word the boy doesn't even know yet, and then later the new house will be his grandma's basement. The boy will lose the catalogs on one moving day or another, but by then he won't need their physical presence. He will have memorized them completely. They will be part of who he is. As he grows, he will make friends and then lose friends, realizing a year or two later that he is unable to remember their names or faces but can still recount the number of bedrooms in their houses, how many bathrooms and a half they had. When he thinks of his old house, the one he had been born in and his mother had died in, he will picture it as a spread in one of his catalogs, imaginary fingers tracing the picture of the remembered home, the hard blue lines of the floor plans.

Home: Three bedrooms. One bath. Storm windows and a thirty-five-year guarantee on the shingles.

Family: Two parents. One child. One dead with two survivors.

This is a home. This is a family. This is what happens in a home when a family breaks down a fault line, when a foundation suddenly shifts because once it got wet when it should have stayed dry, because that wet spot was sealed beneath the floorboards, because it hid there for years and years before cracks began showing around doorways and windows, before one day whole chunks of plaster fell from the ceilings and walls as something fundamental within gave way to ruin.

THE COLLECTORS

| 1A. HOMER STANDS, FALLS, STANDS AGAIN |

How long has Homer been sitting here in the dark? A decade, a year, a day, an hour, a minute, or at least this minute, the one where his eyes pop open and his ears perk up, listening to the voice howling in the dark. Somewhere in the house, Langley is yelling for Homer to help him, has, perhaps, been doing so for some time. Homer leans over the edge of his tattered leather chair—the chair that once belonged to his father and has been his home since he lost his sight—then sets down his snifter, the brandy long ago emptied into the hollows of his throat. He stands, legs shaky, and for a moment thinks he will fall back into the chair's ripped excess. He finds his balance, takes a step or two forward, then loses it, crashing forward onto the damp floor covered in orange peels and pipe ash, the remains of the only forms of nourishment he's allowed. Homer calls out for Langley, who calls out for him, and together their voices echo through the twisted passageways and piled junk of their home. Homer's eyes long gone, everything has become touch, life a mere series of tactile experiences. He pushes himself upward, his hands sinking into the orange peels that litter the floor, their consistency like gums pulled away from teeth. He's disgusted, but has been for so many years that this newest indignity barely registers.

In a loud voice, he tells Langley that he is coming, but he doesn't know if that's true. There's so much between them, much of it dangerous, all of it theirs.

| 3A. INVENTORY |

Some of the items removed from the Collyer mansion include hundreds of feet of rope, three baby carriages, rakes and hoes and other gardening implements, several rusted bicycles, kitchen utensils (including at least four complete sets of china and several potato peelers), a heap of glass chandeliers that had been removed from the ceilings to make room for the piles and the tunnels, the folding top of a horse-drawn carriage, a sawhorse, a room full of dressmaking dummies, several portraits of both family members and early-century presidents such as Calvin Coolidge and Warren Harding, a plaster bust of Herman Melville, a kerosene stove placed precariously close to the stacks of newspapers in Homer's sitting room, a variety of children's furniture and clothing, the chassis of a Model T Ford that Langley had apparently been trying to turn into a generator, hundreds of yards of unused silk and other fabrics, several broken clocks and piles of clock parts, one British and six American flags, piles of tapestries and rugs, whole rooms filled with broken furniture and bundled lumber. There was also the matter of their inheritance from their father, which included all his medical equipment, plus his thousands of medical and anatomical reference texts, greatly expanding the already large, impenetrably stuffed Collyer family library. All in all, the accumulated possessions of the Collyer brothers added up to over one hundred fifty tons of junk, most of it unremarkable except for the advanced state of ruin and decay that infused everything.

There were also eight cats, an emaciated dog, and countless numbers of vermin. By the time Langley was found, the rats had eaten most of his face and extremities and the cockroaches were beginning to carry off the rest.

| 2A. THOSE WHO CAME FOR YOU FIRST |

It began with the newspapermen, their tales of the gold stashed in your halls, of stockpiled gems and expensive paintings and antique jewelry. None of it was true, but none of it surprised you either. The reporters have never worried about the truth before, not when it came to you and yours.

So the articles run, and then they come: not your true neighbors, but these new ones who replaced them. The first brick through the window is merely irritating, the second more so, but by the third and the fourth you've had enough and board up all the windows. You have to go out at night and scavenge more wood despite Homer's protests, his pleas for you to use the piles of lumber already in the house. He doesn't understand that what you have gathered already has purpose, is stock against future tragedies.

The bricks are only precursors, warnings: There is a break-in, and then another. The first time you fire a gun in the house, Homer screams for two days, refusing to calm down no matter what you say. You count yourself lucky that he's gone blind, or else he might have come down himself, seen the blood soaked into the piles of newspapers bordering the basement door.

Afterward, you move even more bundles to the basement, stacking newspaper to the ceiling, layering it six feet deep. Heavy and damp and covered in mold and rot, you know that no burglar will be able to push his way through the newsprint. It is your family's history that they are after, the city's that will keep them out.

| 4A. HOW I CAME IN |

I came in through a history of accumulation, through a trail of documents that led to you, Langley, and to him, Homer. I came in through the inventory of your home, through the listing of objects written down as if they meant something, as if they were clues to who you are.

Obsessed, I filled one book and then another and then another.

What I learned was that even a book can be a door if you hold it right, and I held it right.

When I arrived at your home, I did not climb the steps or knock on your door. Instead, I waited and watched and when you came out I followed behind you.

I watched your flight through the dark night air, watched as you pretended skittishness in the streets. I followed you from backyard to alley to dumpster, lingered behind as you scavenged for food and pump-drawn water and shiny objects to line your halls. I watched you take each new prize and clutch it to your breast, and when you were ready to return, I followed you inside.

I want to tell you now that I am a night bird too, just another breed of crow.

Like the bird we each resemble, I am both a scavenger of what has happened and an omen of what is to come.

Despite your fears, I am not your death.

Despite this assurance, you will not be saved.

I promise you, I will be here with you when you fall, and when he fails.

After you are both gone, I am afraid that I will still be here.

| 3B. INVENTORY |

Thirty Harlem phone books, one for each year from 1909 to 1939: Individually, they are just another pile of junk, but read as a collection they are something else. The names change from Roosevelt to Robeson, from Fitzgerald to Hughes, a process that doesn't happen all at once but slowly, like the mixing after a blood infusion. By the 1920s, Miller and Audubon and Rockwell are gone, replaced by Armstrong and Ellington and DuBois. Read like this, they are yet another type of wall, one that is both harder to see and yet obvious enough once you know the color of the bricks.

| 1B. HOMER HATES THE WEATHER IN NEW YORK CITY |

When it rains, water comes in through the ceiling, creates trickling waterfalls that cascade downward from floor to floor, from pile to pile. The wood of every chair and table feels warped and cracked while nearby newspaper bundles grow heavy with mold and dampness that will never leave, their pages slippery with the ink leaking downward into the carpet. Things float in the water, or worse, swim, like the rats and cockroaches and whatever else lives in the high press of the stacks. Other floors are similarly obscured by the often ankle-deep torrents, hiding broken glass, sharp sticks, knives and scalpels, the dozens of light bulbs Langley broke in a fit when the electricity was shut off for nonpayment.

Once, Homer remembers, it snowed in his sitting room, the flakes settling on his face and tongue and clothes. He'd had only Langley's word and the freeze of the air to tell him it was snow that fell that day. Reaching out his tongue, he feared he'd taste ash instead, but said nothing as his brother laughed and refilled their snifters.

| 3C. INVENTORY |

Inside much of the house, the only navigation possible was through tunnels Langley had carved into the piles of garbage that filled each room. Supported with scraps of lumber and stacked newspaper or cardboard, these tunnels appeared to collapse frequently, forcing Langley to start over or to create alternate paths to the parts of the house he wished to access.

Some of the tunnels were wide enough that a person could crawl comfortably through them, and in places even walk in a crouch. Others, especially on the second floor, were much smaller. Langley might have been able to fit through them, but not the heavier Homer. The tunnels were the closest thing the house had to doors, and beyond them were secrets the older brother had most likely not shared in decades.

Langley once claimed to be saving the newspapers so that when his brother regained his sight he would be able to catch up on the news. It wasn't a funny joke, but Langley wasn't a funny man. The earliest newspapers in the house date from 1933, the year Homer went blind, and they continued to be delivered until weeks after the house began to be emptied and inventoried. Even allowing for twelve years of uninterrupted delivery, there were still far more newspapers in the house than anyone could have expected. They were stacked and bundled in every room, in every hall, covering the landings of staircases and filled closets and chests. Even if Homer had somehow learned to see again, this was never going to be the best way to rejoin the world.

| 1C. HOMER TAKES HIS MEDICINE |

After Homer had lost his sight, his brother put him on a diet of nothing but oranges, convinced the fruit would restore his vision. Homer wasn't so sure, but he couldn't go out and get food himself—only Langley ever left the mansion, and even then only at night—and so Homer had no choice but to take what was offered. Every day, he ate a dozen oranges, until his breath stank of rind and pulp, until the undersides of his fingernails were crusted with the sticky leftovers of his meals. Langley told him that if he could eat one hundred oranges a week his sight would come back, but Homer couldn't do it, no matter how hard he tried. It was too much of one thing, a deadening of his taste buds as complete as the deadening of his irises, his corneas, his optic nerves that still sent useless signals down the rotted pathways of his all too useless brain.

| 2B. THE ONLY THING YOU HAVE CAUGHT THUS FAR |

You started making the booby traps after the break-ins began, and never stopped revising and improving this new class of inventions. You rigged tripwires and deadfalls, hid walls of sharpened broomsticks behind the moist surface of your newspaper tunnels. Poured loose piles of broken glass beneath intentionally weakened floorboards. Made other traps and then forgot them, until you were unsure about even your own safety.

More and more, you had to tell Homer that maybe the best thing for him would be to stay in his chair.

The one that got you was a tripwire in the second-story hallway leading from the staircase to the master bedroom. You were hurrying, careless for one moment, just long enough to trip the wire that released the trap, burying you beneath a manmade boulder, a netted mass of typewriters and sewing machines and bowling balls hung from the ceiling months before.

Even with all that coming toward you, you almost got away. Only your right leg is pinned and broken, but that is all it takes to doom you. You cannot see behind you well enough to know how bad the wound is, but even through the mold and must you smell the blood leeched from your body, soaking the already-ruined hallway carpet.

| 1D. HOMER IS MERCIFUL |

It doesn't take long for Homer to lose his bearings and get lost, turning randomly at each intersection in the tunnels. Without sight, there's no way to check the few clues that might yet remain, like the pattern on the ceiling or the moldings in the corners. He reaches out with his hands, stretches his fingers toward whatever awaits them, every inch a lifetime's worth of danger. The space is filled with tree branches, a bramble slick with rot and sticky with sap. Homer recoils at the sound of movement nearby—insect or rodent or reptile, Homer can't know which—and with his next step he crushes something beneath his foot, the snap of a vertebrae or carapace muffled by the sheer bulk of the room. He stops for a moment to stamp the thing out, to be sure it is dead. Somewhere his brother moans in the stacks, and there's no reason for whatever creature lies beneath his heel to suffer the same.

| 2C. JUSTIFYING YOUR GATHERING |

When your father left you and your brother and your mother, he took everything with him. He took his medical books and his anatomical drawings and his specimen jars. He took his suits and his shoes and his hats. He took his golf clubs and his pipes and his records, and when he was gone, your mother scrubbed the house from top to bottom in her grief, removing every last particle of dust that might once have been him. He left her, and in return she eradicated him so thoroughly that for twenty years he stayed out of the house.

And then he returned, bundled in the back of a truck and disguised as gynecological equipment and ornate furniture, as something that could be bound into chests and sacks and bundles of paper.

He took everything that might have been yours, and just because it eventually came back doesn't mean you didn't hurt during the years it was gone. Now you have him trapped, boarded behind the doors of the second floor, and he will never escape again. Every stray hair still clinging to a shirt collar, every scrap of handwriting left in the margins of his texts, all of it is him, is who he was. It is all that's left, but if you keep it safe then it is all you'll ever need.

| 3D. INVENTORY |

The master bedroom was found full of correspondence, tied into bundles organized by month and year. The letters begin arriving in 1909, then increased in frequency during the following decade until a letter arrived almost every single day. After this peak, the correspondence slowly tapers off before stopping in 1923. The bulk of the unopened mail is from Herman Collyer, each letter a single entry in a series of entreaties dating from his abandonment of his family to the year of his own death. Whether Langley ever showed his brother these sealed envelopes is open to debate, but his own stance on his father's writings is more definitive: Each letter remained an apology unasked for, unwanted and unopened, from the day they were received until the day he died.

| 2D. THE FIRST HOARD |

Was inherited, not gathered. Your father died and suddenly all his possessions were yours, spilling out of your rooms and into your halls. As if you knew what to do with the evidence of a lifetime. As if you could throw away your father, or sell him off to strangers.

It wasn't long after that when you started adding to the piles yourself, was it?

If only you gathered enough, then maybe you could build a father. Gather a mother up in your arms, like all these piles of porcelain knick-knacks. Design a family from things best left behind. Replace birth with theft, life with hoarding, death with destruction. This house is a body, and you and Homer move within it. Rooms like cells, floors like organs, and you two—like what, exactly? Pulses of electricity, nervous messages, the tiny sparks that one day might bring this place to life?

Listen—

Somewhere, Homer is crying again, isn't he?

| 4B. WHERE I AM IN RELATION TO WHERE YOU ARE |

The thin biography tells me nothing, doesn't help me penetrate past the birth and death dates, the one extant photograph, the mere facts of your father leaving you and of your mother dying and of the great divide opened between you and your brother by his blindness. I am divided from you too, by decades I could not cross in time. The only way I feel close to you is when I read the list of objects you left behind, because I know that in your needy acquisitions there is something of me.

Are you listening?

Breathe, Langley. *Breathe.*

| 1E. HOMER REMEMBERS HIS FACE |

Homer crawls on his hands and knees, searching for signs of his brother, whose voice is a cricket's, always out of reach, the sound coming from every direction at once. Homer is hungry and tired and wants to go back to his chair, but he perseveres. His brother would do it for him. His brother has been doing it for him. On each of the thousands of days since Homer went blind, Langley has fed him and clothed him and kept him company—has kept him safe from the intruders Homer isn't supposed to talk about—and now on the day when Langley needs his help, he is failing. Homer's face is wet but he doesn't know if the wetness is tears or sweat or something else, something dripping from the ceiling and the stacks. He doesn't think he's crying but feels he might start soon, might start and never stop. Whatever it is, he doesn't reach up to wipe it away. His hands are filthy, filthier than anything that might be there on his face.

His face: Once, before his blindness but after he stopped being able to look himself in the mirror, Homer dreamed he was a man made of mud, a pillar of dust, some delicate creation waiting to be dispersed or destroyed.

It was just a dream, he knows, not motivation or reason for staying in his chair as long as he has. Not the cause of his nothingman life. He wishes he could go back, forget he ever left the chair, ever left the sitting room, ever reentered the world of pain that had always been there waiting for him. His bathrobe is torn, his hands and feet bloodied and bruised, and his face—

Over the years, he has forgotten his face, the shape of the thing, the angle of his nose and the thickness of his lips and the scars or lack of scars that might distinguish it from another. He has forgotten how it feels to see a brow furrow in pain, to see a mouth contort in frustration and anger.

He has forgotten, but he is trying to remember.

Whatever his face is, floating in the dark around his eyes, it is wet again.

| 3E. INVENTORY |

Fourteen pianos, both grand and upright. A clavichord, two organs, six banjos, a dozen violins (only two of which are strung), bugles, accordions, a gramophone and an exhaustive record collection (including well-worn works by Paul Whiteman, Fred Waring, Sophie Tucker, and Blossom Seeley), two trumpets, a trombone, and what appears to have once been an upright bass before it was smashed and broken. Both brothers were accomplished musicians, and it is easy to picture them sitting and playing music together, and later, after the lights went out and they began to fight, apart from each other, their only points of connection the accidental melodies they made in the dark.

| 1F. HOMER PLAYS THE PIANO |

After Homer trips over the bench in front of the parlor's piano, he sits down and rests his fingers on the keys. Wherever Langley is, he's quiet, resting too, or else something worse, something Homer doesn't want to think about. He feels bad enough, for not hurrying, for not being able to find his brother and save him.

His lungs ache and his ankles throb, the arthritis in his leg joints a lightless fire. He centers himself in front of the piano and starts to play, then stops when the sound comes out wrong. He sighs, starts over with more realistic expectations.

The piano is almost completely buried by the mounds of trash that fill the room, the heaps of paper and metal and wood, the objects breaking down again into their constituent parts. Homer's fingers are gnarled ghosts, flickering over the keys in an approximation, the memory of music. The sound comes out of the piano muffled and muted. It does not fill the room but goes into it instead, Homer's fingers driving each note through the piled garbage and into the rotting walls like a nail, like a crowbar, like something meant to hold a thing together, like something meant to tear it down.

| 4C. MOTIVATION |

I'm sifting through their possessions, crawling through the ruins of their lives searching for those lost, for remains, for the remains of a family: I am in the master bedroom, reading letters they never read. I am in the parlor, wiping the grime off a generation of portraits. I am in the hallway, setting thousands of mouse traps all in a row.

I am on my hands and knees, scrubbing the floor without success, as if there could ever be enough soap to remove this particular stain.

There is so much to see here, but only in fragments, in peripheries. Every step across the floorboards brings this house of cards closer to collapse, and so I must move backward and forward in time, balancing the now and the then, until I have found what it is I am looking for.

I am a collector too, but it is not their possessions I have clutched close and hoarded.

I am holding Homer's face in my hands, staring into his milky eyes, whispering to him as he searches in starved sadness. I am kneeling beside Langley like a detective, my bent knee slick with his blood, looking through the rote clues to discover what happened to him.

I am conducting an investigation. I am holding a wake. I am doing some or all or none of these things.

| 2E. THE CRACK IN YOUR FOUNDATION |

You howl, hurling the curse of your brother's name down the corridor. For hours you have heard his bumbling and still he is no closer to you, his blind search for you as failed as your own cursed attempt to reach the master bedroom. You picture him crawling forward on his hands and knees, unable to see through to the end of each tunnel, unable to know how much farther there is still to go.

For years, he has kept to his chair in the sitting room, leaving you to deal with the collapse of the house, the danger it poses to all of your possessions. The house is both protector and destroyer, both safety and threat, and it is you who tips the scales, not him. It was you who braved the streets night after night to bring back food and water, to gather all the supplies essential to your lives. Homer knows nothing of what you've had to do, how you've moved from one halo of lamp light to the next, avoiding the dark men who rule the streets. You see their eyes sometimes in the shadows, peering at you from front steps and street corners, hurrying you on your way through this ruined city that was once your home.

The pain is too much. This time when you scream, your brother answers, but from too far away. The slow sticky warmth emanating from your crushed thigh has reached your crotch, your belly. It's easy to reach down and feel the slippery copper heat of your blood. There's so much, more than you expected.

You close your eyes. Not much longer now.

Even surrounded by all your possessions, dying is so much lonelier than you expected.

Whisper your brother's name. Whisper the names of your father and your mother. Whisper my name, and pray that I might save you, but understand that even though I have already changed the truth merely by being here, I will still refuse to change it that much.

| 1G. HOMER LOSES FAITH |

The house bucks and shudders, settles or shifts. Homer stumbles but doesn't fall down, knows that if he does he might never get up. He stops and listens to the creaking of the floorboards, the scuttle of the rats. Says, Langley?

Homer wants to yell his brother's name again but doesn't. It's been a long time since his brother answered, and without sight there is no light and no marker of time. Homer doesn't know if it's morning or night, if a few hours have passed or if it's already been days. He's so tired and so alone, lost inside his own house, remade in whatever crooked shape Langley has envisioned. He thinks about all Langley tells him when to do because he cannot tell himself.

Homer, go to sleep, it's midnight.

Homer, wake up, I've got your breakfast.

Homer, it's time to play your violin.

It's time for me to read to you.

It's time for a drink, time for a smoke, time to eat another orange.

Homer's so tired, and all he wants is to be back in his chair, but for once Langley needs his help and Homer doesn't want to let his brother down.

The thing is, he doesn't know if Langley is still there to be helped.

| 2F. YOUR WEIGHTY GHOSTS |

No father without medicine, without dictionaries, without reference texts full of once perfect answers slowly rotting themselves wrong.

No mother without silk, without satin, without wool and cotton. No mother without a closet full of shoes, a hundred high heels spilled out into a trapped nest of spikes.

No brother without a piano, without a bathrobe, without a chair, a pipe, a mouthful of oranges and black bread.

No self without these ghosts.

No ghosts, without—

No. No ghosts, or rather:

No ghosts except in things.

They surround you, press closer, waiting for the rapidly approaching moment when you too will be just a thing, an object, a static entity slowly falling into decay. That moment is so close you can smell it, like the breath of rats, like the rot of oranges, like blood and dirt mushed into new mud.

| 4D. MARCH 21 (EARLY) |

I know you were hurrying through the second floor hall because you knew what you needed to do to complete this place, to bring an end to the endless gathering and piling and sorting. You were hurrying because it had taken you so long already, and you didn't want to waste another second.

Even now, at the very end, you tell yourself that if only you could have completed your project then it would have been enough to stop all this. It could have been different. You could have taken Homer and left this house. You could have started over somewhere else, which is all you've ever wanted.

You were hurrying, and you were careless, and now it's too late.

Your lungs heave, trying unsuccessfully to clear their bloody fractures. When you are still again, I reach down to touch your face, to turn it toward my own.

With my fingers twisted around your jaw, I say, Homer isn't coming.

I say, Tell me what you would have told him.

I can see the sparks dancing in your eyes, obscuring the last sights you'll ever see, so I say, Close your eyes. You don't need them anymore. Not for how little is left.

For these last few moments, I will see for you as you saw for him.

In the last seconds of your life, I will tell you whatever you want to hear, as long as you first tell me what I need.

I say, Tell me how to finish the house.

I say, Tell me what I have to do to get out of here.

And then you will, and afterward I will lie to you, and despite my whispered assurances you will know that I am not real enough to save you or him, and then it will be over.

| 1H. HOMER FINDS THE FARTHEST ROOM |

Homer experiences the lack of guideposts, of landmarks, of bread crumbs. He knows his brother is dead or dying and that finding him will change nothing, and even though he wants to turn around he's not sure how. He tries to remember if he climbed the stairs or if he crawled upward or if he is still on the first floor of the house, twisted and turned inside it. He tries to remember the right and the left, the up and the down, the falls and the getting back up, but when he does the memories come all at once or else as one static image of moving in the dark, like a claustrophobia of neurons. He wants to lie down upon on the floor, wants to stop this incessant, wasted movement.

He closes his eyes and leans against the piles. His breath comes long and ragged, whole rooms of air displaced by the straining bellows of his lungs. He smells the long dormant stench of his sweat and piss and shit, come shamefully back to life now that he's on the move again.

Somewhere beyond himself, he smells, if he sniffs hard enough, just a hint of his orange peels, the last of their crushed sweetness.

Homer opens his eyes, useless as they are, and points himself toward the wafting rot of his last thousand meals. He holds his robe closed with one hand, reaches out with the other toward the dark. He puts one foot in front of the other, then smiles when he feels the rinds and tapped ash begin to squish between his toes.

He slips, and falls, and crashes into the tortured leather of his favorite chair. He pulls himself up. He sits himself down. He puts his heavy head into his hands.

| 3F. INVENTORY |

In the lock box: Thirty-four bank books, all from different banks. Irving Trust Company. Fillmore-Leroy. Liberty National. Park Avenue. Seaboard. Albany City Savings. Temple Beth Israel. Alfred Mutual. ABN. Alliance. Amalgated. American Bond and Mortgage. Jefferson Savings. Associated Water Companies Credit Union. Assumption Parish. Canaseraga State. Dry Dock. Eighth Avenue. Fallkill. Queens County. Glaser Mercantile. H&K. Village. Industrial Bank of Ithaca. Kings County. Manhattan Trust. State Dime Savings. Bank of Brooklyn. Oneida. Rockaway. Union National Bank of Friendship. Beacon Federal. Whitehall Trust. The Zurich Depository.

A total of three thousand dollars and eighteen cents. The very end of a fortune, kept in Langley's name, inherited by Homer, and then, after he died too, taken by the state.

Homer squirms on the high throne of his last decade, every pose the wrong one. His back aches and his legs jerk no matter how he adjusts himself. Everything is physical, every craving desire a need for his brother, for his abandoned Langley. Homer would give everything away for a glass of water, would go into equal debt for a snifter of brandy or a pipe or even one of Langley's goddamn oranges. Anything that might bring relief. Anything that might bring with it absolution or forgetfulness. He licks his lips and tastes mud. He puts his fingers to his mouth and sucks and there it is again. His face, his beard, his clothes, all are mud. Homer puts his hand back in his mouth, sucks and swallows until it is clean. He repeats the process with his other hand, and then he cleans himself like a rodent, using his hands to bring the dirt off of his face and neck and arms to his mouth, where he devours it. Homer's throat chokes shut. He closes his eyes to block out the last blurs of gauzy light his blindness still allows. He is inside the house and the house is inside him, like a nesting of labyrinths. Lacking the tools to solve himself, he gives up. The process starts in this one second but takes weeks to finish. He does not cry out again. He does not beg. He does not want, not for food or water or companionship. He could, but he does not. This life has been an abject lesson in the limits of wanting, and he has learned all he cares to learn.

| 5A. WILLIAM BAKER |

William Baker breaks a second-story window from atop a shaking ladder. William Baker peers into the darkness and then signals to the other officers that he's going in. William Baker uses his nightstick to clear all the glass out of his way. William Baker climbs through the window into the room beyond. William Baker gags but does not vomit. William Baker turns his flashlight from left to right, then back again, like a lighthouse in a sea of trash. William Baker thinks, Not a sea but a mountain rising from a sea, a new, unintended landscape. William Baker begins to take inventory in his mind, counting piles of newspapers, broken furnishings, books molded to floorboards. William Baker puts his hands to a wall of old newspapers and pushes until he sinks in to his wrists. William Baker finds the entrance to the tunnel that leads out of the room, then gets down on his hands and knees and crawls through. William Baker passes folding chairs and sewing machines and a wine press. William Baker passes the skeleton of a cat or else a rat as big as a cat. William Baker turns left at a baby carriage, crawls over a bundle of old umbrellas. William Baker crawls until he can't hear the other officers yelling to him from the window. William Baker is inside the house, inside its musty, rotted breath, inside its tissues of decaying paper and wood.

William Baker disappears from the living world and doesn't come back until two hours later, when he appears at the window with his face blanched so white it shines in the midnight gloom. William Baker knows where Homer Collyer's body is. William Baker has held the dead man, has lifted him from his death chair as if the skin and bones and tattered blue and white bathrobe still constituted a human person, someone worth saving. William Baker counts the seconds that pass, the minutes, the days and the years. William Baker thinks it took a long time for this man to die. William Baker has no idea.

| 5B. ARTIE MATTHEWS |

Artie Matthews doesn't understand how a house can smell so bad throughout every inch of its frame. Artie Matthews thinks the garbage should have blocked the smell at some point. Artie Matthews smells it on the sidewalk, smells it in the foyer, smells it in the rooms he and the other workers have cleared and he smells it in the rooms they haven't. Artie Matthews wears coveralls and boots and thick leather gloves and a handkerchief over his face and wonders if it's enough to protect him from what happened here. Artie Matthews has arms that ache and knees that tremble from yesterday's exertions as he climbs the stairs to the second floor. Artie Matthews throws cardboard and newspaper out a window. Artie Matthews throws out armfuls of books that reek of mold and wet ink. Artie Matthews pushes a dresser to the window and empties its contents onto the lawn below. Artie Matthews wonders who these clothes belong to, wonders if there is a wife or a mother or someone else still trapped in the house, or if this woman left long ago. Her brassieres and slips and skirts fall to the ground. Artie Matthews watches another worker trying to gather them up before the pressing crowds can see them. Artie Matthews wonders why the worker is bothering, why anyone would worry that the people who lived in this house have any dignity left to protect. Artie Matthews thinks that what they are really removing from the house is shame made tangible as wood and steel and fabric.

Artie Matthews will find Langley Collyer, but not for two more weeks. Artie Matthews will find him buried beneath a deadfall of trash ten feet from where his brother died and wonder why he didn't yell, why he didn't ask Homer for help. Artie Matthews will not realize that Langley did yell, did howl, did scream and cajole and beg and whimper. Artie Matthews will not be able to hear how sound moved in this house before all the walls and tunnels of trash came down. Artie Matthews will never understand how a man might cry out for help only to have his last words get lost in the deep labyrinth he's made of his life.

| 3G. INVENTORY |

Besides the letters, there was one final object found in the master bedroom, hidden beneath a canvas tarp. It is a model, a doll house, a scaled approximation of the brownstone home. Inside, the model's smooth wood floors are stained and then carpeted, the walls all papered or painted with care. There is an intricately carved staircase that winds to the second floor, its splendor shaming its murderous real-life counterpart. Tiny paintings hang on the walls, painstaking recreations of the smeared and slashed portraits found downstairs. Miniature chandeliers dangle from the ceilings in nearly every room.

There are tiny beds, tiny tables and chairs, tiny pianos. There are even tiny books with tiny pages and a violin so small that it would take a pair of tweezers to hold its bow.

In the downstairs sitting room, there is a tiny version of what Homer's chair must have looked like before the leather tore open, before its stuffing leaked onto the floor.

This is a house without traps, without tunnels and stacks and collections that never seem complete.

In the absence of photographs, this is perhaps the closest thing to the truth of who these people used to be.

The wood floor around the model gleams, its surface scrubbed and polished, contrasting with the filth and rot of the rest of the room, left unprotected by the tarp.

Outside this circle, there are dozens of prototypes for what would have been the model's finishing touches: Four figures, repeated over and over in different mediums. A man and a woman and two small boys, rendered from wood and clay and string and straw and hair and other, less identifiable materials. All discarded, cast aside, and no more a family than anything else we found lying upon the floors of the Collyer House.

| 4E. DECAY |

I wanted to leave after both of you were dead, or at least after your bodies were bagged and covered and taken out into the sunlight that awaited you, that had always been waiting. Instead, I remain here, walking these emptying halls. Without you to talk to, I become desperate for connection, for these workers tearing down your tunnels to see what you had become, what you might have been instead. I tap a new father on the shoulder so that he turns and sees the child's mobile hanging in a newly opened space, its meaning slanted by your own childlessness. I open a medical reference text to the page on treatments for rheumatoid arthritis or diabetic blindness, then leave it on top of the stack for someone else to read, to note what is absent, to see that nowhere on the page is the cure of the hundred oranges you prescribed your brother. I whisper explanations into curious ears, explain that what you had planned to do with all these piles of lumber was to build a house inside the house, to build a structure capable of holding a family together, something the previous one had failed to do.

I try to explain to them how close you were, how close I am, how with a little more help I could solve this puzzle, but they don't understand. They are not trying to understand you.

They are trying to throw you away, and they are succeeding.

Before they finish, I go up to each nameless sanitation worker and offer him a facet of your lives, a single dusty jewel plucked from the thousands you had gathered.

To each person, I try to give the thing he has been looking for, to offer him a history of you that will clash with the official version, with the version of the facts already being assembled by the historians and newspapermen. I want them to see you as I wanted to see you when I first came to this place, before I started telling your story to my own ends.

* * *

I leave minutes ahead of the wrecking ball. All your possessions have been carted away to be burned, or else tied into garbage bags and discarded. What took you decades to acquire took other men mere weeks to throw away, and now all that you were is gone. Despite the many opportunities to take whatever I wanted, I have left all of your possessions behind, with only a few exceptions: I have taken one of Homer's orange peels, with hopes that it might help me see, and I have taken the makings of one of your traps, on the off-chance that it might protect me better than it did you. I have left everything else for the historians and garbage men to do with what they will. The workers want to throw you away, but the historians who follow will want something else altogether. They will gather you into inventories, into feature articles and well-researched biographies. They will annotate and organize. They will hoard the facts, organizing them into timelines and tight paragraphs of passive prose, then publish their theories in journals and books before reciting them on television shows and in packed lecture halls. They will collect more of you and Homer than anyone should need or want, and then they will collect some more, never satisfied with what they have, always greedy for more facts and more theories.

Once, I wanted to be just like them.

Once, I too built a trap for myself out of a few obsessed pages, and when I fell in, it crushed me too. Sometimes I am still there, calling out for help to anyone who will listen.

AN INDEX OF HOW
OUR FAMILY WAS KILLED

A brother, a father, a mother, a sister.

A family, to begin with.

A family, whatever that is.

A list of evidence, compiled in alphabetical order rather than in order of importance, rather than in the order in which I gathered these clues.

A message, left on my answering machine and never deleted: My sister's voice, telling me she's okay, that she's still there.

Absence of loved ones, never diminishing no matter how much time has passed.

Accidents happen, but what happened to us was not an accident.

Acquittal, but not for them, and not for us.

Alarms that failed to go off, that have never stopped ringing in my ears.

Alibis, as in, everyone's got one.

Ambulances that never arrive in time to save anyone.

An index, a collection of echoes, each one suggesting a whole only partially sensed.

Arrest, to bring into custody.

Arrest, to bring to a stop.

Autopsy, as a means of discovering the cause of death.

Axe, as possibility. Also, other sharp objects, other combinations of handles and blades.

Ballistics, as method of investigation.

Blood, scrubbed from the floor of bedrooms and barrooms and hospital beds, sometimes by myself, more often by others, by strangers, by men and women in white clothes, unaffected by the crime at hand.

Brother, memory of: Once, my brother and I built a fort in the woods behind our house by digging a pit and covering it with plywood. Once, we put the neighbor kid down in that pit and covered the hole. Once, we listened to him scream for hours from the back porch, where we ate cookies and milk and misunderstood what it was we were doing wrong.

Brother, murdered. Murdered by a woman, a wife, his wife, the wife he had left but not divorced. Who he had left for another woman, a woman who could not protect him even with a house clasped tight with locks. Murdered in his sleep, with a blade to the eye. Murdered beside his new woman, who woke up screaming and didn't stop for days.

Bruises so black I couldn't recognize her face, couldn't be sure when I told the coroner that yes, this is my mother.

Bullets, general, fear thereof.

Bullets, specific: One lodged in my father's sternum, another passing through skin and tissue and lung, puncturing his last hot gasp of air.

Bullets, specific: Pieces of lead, twin mushrooms clattering in a clear film canister. Sometimes I shake them like dice, like bones, but when I pour them out onto my desk they tell me nothing, their prophecy limited to that which has already come.

Call me once a day, just to let me know you're still safe.

Call me X, if you have to call me anything at all.

Camera, fear of, need for. To document the bodies, to show the size and location of wounds, to produce photographs to explain the entry and exit points of weapons.

Car accidents, as in, it is easier to say that it was a car accident than to tell our friends what really happened.

Caskets, closed.

Control, impossibility of.

Crimes, solved: Murders of father, mother, brother.

Crimes, uncommitted (and therefore as yet unsolved):
   Murder of sister, murder of self.

Curse, as possible explanation.

Do not.

Do not ask for assistance.

Do not associate with one-armed men, men with tattoos, men with bad teeth or bad breath or bad dispositions.

Do not answer the phone.

Do not be the messenger, for they are often shot.

Do not believe everything you hear.

Do not break down on the side of the road.

Do not call out for help—Yell FIRE instead. It will not save you, but at least there will be witnesses.

Do not cheat at cards or darts or pool.

Do not cheat on your spouse.

Do not cross the street without looking.

Do not date, no matter how lonely you get.

Do not disagree with people with loud voices or short fuses.

Do not discuss religion or politics.

Do not drink in bars.

Do not dress in flashy or revealing clothes. Do not ask for it.

Do not fight for custody of your children. Better they see you one weekend a month than in a casket.

Do not fly in airplanes.

Do not forget that you are destined for death, that your family carries doom like a fat bird around its neck, that it is something you will never be rid of.

Do not forget to set the alarm when you leave the house, when you go to sleep at night.

Do not fuck around.

Do not get divorced.

Do not get in fights, in bars or otherwise.

Do not get married.

Do not go looking for trouble.

Do not go outside at night or during the day.

Do not go skinny dipping in dark ponds with anyone.

Do not hire a private detective. They may find what you are looking for, but they will also find out about you.

Do not hitchhike or pick up hitchhikers.

Do not have acquaintances.

Do not have friends.

Do not hope too much.

Do not leave trails of breadcrumbs showing which way you have gone.

Do not leave your phone number written in match books or on cocktail napkins.

Do not linger outside of buildings. Do not smoke or wait for busses or cabs.

Do not look back when you should be running away.

Do not love a man with a temper.

Do not love men at all, or women either.

Do not make enemies, if you can help it.

Do not meet strange men or women you find on the internet in coffee shops or bars or motels.

Do not play with fire.

Do not pray for salvation, for protection, for deliverance.

Do not push your luck.

Do not put your trust in security guards, in the police arriving on time.

Do not raise your voice in anger.

Do not sleep, for as long as you can avoid it.

Do not smoke marijuana, as you are paranoid enough already.

Do not take any drugs at all.

Do not take shortcuts.

Do not take the same way home twice.

Do not telegraph your punches.

Do not telephone home and say you'll be out all night.

Do not think that not doing any of these things will be
enough to save you.

Evidence as symbol of a crime committed, of a
deed done.

Evidence, locked away in locked cabinets inside
locked rooms.

Evidence, not harmless, even behind all those locks
and doors.

Ex-wives, as likely suspects.

Eye, as in, keep an eye out. As in, keep your eyes peeled.

Eye, as point of entry, as wound.

Eyewitnesses, reliable enough for the courts, but not
for me. They never tell me what I need to know.

F, tattooed on my left bicep, the first initial of a father lost.

Family, as in mother and father and brother and sister and me.

Family, as something broken and lost.

Family, as something destroyed by external forces deadly as tornados, destructive as wildfires.

Fate, as explanation, as probable cause.

Father, memory of: Always I see my father walking out doors. I see him shutting the door to my bedroom, refusing to leave the light on, even after he gave me something to be afraid of. I see him shutting the car door, locking me in for delirious summer hours while he drank, sitting near a window so he could keep an eye on me. I see him walking out the front door of our house, suitcase in hand, vanishing forever.

Father, murdered. Gunned down by a complete stranger, outside a bar, in Bay City, Michigan. They had not been fighting, nor had they even spoken, at least according to the murderer. This murderer, he said he didn't know why he did it, why he felt compelled to pull the pistol out of his jacket and shoot my father dead. We didn't know either. We hadn't talked to our father in five years, didn't even know he was still in Michigan, waiting to be killed.

Fingerprints are hard to get a hold of, but not impossible. I have spent a fortune to get these cards, these five-fingered imprints of the men and women who have torn my family to shreds. I have placed my own fingers over theirs, but they do not match. I am not accountable, at least not in this most surface of ways.

Fingerprints: Once you know your own, you can dust your house, can prove that no one has been there but you.

Fire, as possibility, since it did not claim any of the others.

Forensics, as method of investigation.

Girlfriend, brother's. Calls over and over, crying into the phone. One reason to get Caller ID.

Guardian angels, non-existent, as far as I can tell.

Gunpowder, smell of: My father's face, when I bent down to kiss him in his coffin.

Hair samples, stored in plastic bags inside folded manila envelopes. Labeled with name, date, relationship. Fragile, dangerous to handle.

Her, the only one of them that remains.

Her, who has separated herself from me, for her safety, for my own.

History, familial, patriarchal and matriarchal: This is not just us, not just my mother and father and brother and sister and myself. This is uncles killed in poker games, aunts smothered in hospitals.

This is babies exposed in vacant lots and brothers holding sisters underwater until the ripples stop. This is history as an inevitable, relentless tide.

History, of an event, of a series of events.

History, personal and also partial, as in this index.

Hospital: The place we were born, the place we go to die, the place we will be declared dead.

Identity, as in, Can you identify this body? As in, Is this the body of your father/mother/brother?

Identity, as in, If I could identify my sister's future killer, could I stop her murder from taking place?

If I can't have him, no one can. Words overheard but ignored. A lesson about the importance of warning signs.

Index as excavation, as unearthing, as exhumation.

Index, as hope, as last chance.

Index, as how to find what you are looking for.

Index, as method of investigation.

Index, as task, as thing to be completed before I die.

Index, as time capsule, as guide to understanding the collected evidence of a life, of a history, of a family tree.

Index, as understanding, however incomplete.

Inevitability, as a likely end to this story.

Insurance policies, as in, Good luck getting one, if you're me. They never tell you that being from a family of murder victims is a risk factor, but it is.

J, tattooed on the inside of my right wrist, first initial of a brother lost.

Jars, for holding each organ individually after they are weighed and categorized and examined for meaning.

Jars, full of brains and livers and hearts. They will not give these to me, no matter how persistently I ask.

Knife, as weapon, if you hold it right.

Like being torn from the arms of the father.

Like being wrenched from the bosom of the mother.

Like closed caskets, like graves all in a row, like the last two plots, waiting to be dug out and then filled in.

Loss of limbs is less important to those who will not survive than those who have to see what is left.

Love, as necessity.

Love, not nearly enough.

Luck, as in bad luck, for all of us.

Madness, temporary, blinding.

Manslaughter implies that what happened was a mistake. In my family, we do not believe in manslaughter.

Memory, doing the best it can.

Memory, failing to do enough all by itself.

Memory, inconsistent, remembering the wrong events, seeking significance and signs where probably there are none.

Memory: When my brother and my sister and then I went off to school, my mother gave us each a St. Christopher's medallion. When she placed mine around my neck, she told me it would protect me, that it would keep me safe from accidents, from accidental death, as if that was all we had to worry about.

Mirror, the only place I see my father's hairline, my mother's nose, my brother's ears, my sister's thin, frightened lips.

Mother, memory of: Lonely before he left, then worse after. There were men with good jobs and men with no jobs, men with tempers and men with appetites, men who were kind to us and men who used us as punching bags, as whipping posts, as receptacles for all the trash they carried inside themselves. Of all those who have failed to protect our family, she was only the first.

Mother, murdered. Died strapped into the passenger seat of a car, unconscious from a head wound, from a wound to the head. I have heard it said both ways. Her boyfriend—a man she started dating after our father left but before he was dead—thought he had killed her with his fists, but was wrong. It was the drowning after he dumped the car that did it.

Motives are almost the opposites of alibis, but not quite.

Mug shots: One, two, three, all in a row on the wall of my office. A reminder of who they were.

My brother's dog, which I take care of but do not trust. He failed to bark in the night once before, and he could do it again.

Mystery, unsolved, even after all this investigation.

Nothing, as inevitable as an ending.

Nothing: impossible to index, to quantify, to explain.

Over-protectiveness is something you learn, but always too late.

P, tattooed on the left side of my neck, first initial of a mother lost.

Persistence of fate, of karma, of destiny, of a wheel turning and turning, crushing whatever falls beneath its heel.

Phones, both answered and unanswered. Bearers of bad news.

Phones ringing and ringing and ringing.

Photographs, blown up and then cropped until the wounds disappear beyond the borders of the frame.

Photographs, mailed to me from Michigan, of my father's body, as unrecognizable as the distance between us.

Photographs of crime scenes, always the same series of angles, repeated for each murder.

Photographs of my brother, dead before he could scream.

Photographs of my brother's eye, of the knife wound left where it used to be.

Photographs of my brother's lips, pressed together in sleep, then death.

Photographs of my mother's face, bruised and broken.

Photographs of my mother's teeth, on the floor of the car.

Photographs of our family of five, and then of four, and then of three. There are no photographs of our family of two. We do not gather. We do not congregate.

Photographs, plastered like wallpaper until all I can see from my desk are familiar clavicles and jaw lines and hands placed palms up to expose too-short life lines.

Police, as in, I have had my fill of the police.

Poison, a possibility. Must prepare my own food, avoid restaurants, parties, buffets and potlucks.

Pre-meditation, as way of life.

Prevention: See, GOOD FUCKING LUCK.

Questions, how can there not be questions?

Risk, always there is the risk that at any moment one wrong word or action might bring upon we who are left what has already been brought to bear on those who are gone.

Rope: There are so many cruelties that can be done with rope that it is hard to know what to be afraid of.

Search party, looking for my mother, before we knew she'd gone through the surface of the lake.

Sister, memory of: Happy in the fourth grade when she won the school spelling bee. Happy at her confirmation, when God promised to protect her forever. Happy at my brother's wedding, dancing the polka. Happy, happy, happy, until she wasn't happy anymore or ever again.

Sister, survivor. She has tried to live a life free of dangers. She follows every rule, every instruction, takes every precaution. She does not talk to strangers, either men or women. She does not talk to children or babies. She does not pet dogs or hold cats or touch any other small domestic animals. In her purse, she keeps both mace and pepper spray, but she never walks anywhere. She has a tazer in her glove box, but never drives. If she walks or if she drives, then she will die. If she rides in cars with others, then they too will die because she is with them. There are no knives or forks or shovels or tire irons in her house. She does not answer her phone or check her e-mail or open her door, ever, even if it is me knocking. She has done everything she can, but it will not be enough. I have not seen her in months, but that does not mean I believe she is safe. Sooner or later, my phone will ring, and then I will know that she too is gone.

Sometimes, I go to department store perfume counters and spray my mother's scent onto a test card. In the back of my wallet are dozens of these now scentless things, marked only by the splotch stained across the white cardstock.

Sometimes, I think of my father without realizing he's gone, my heart numb as an amputee's fingers, as a lost hand trying to pick up a telephone over and over and over.

Sometimes, while I'm petting my brother's dog, I have to stop myself from hurting it, from punishing it for its failure to bark, to warn, to save its owner's life.

Strangulation, as possibility. To be that close to the killer, to see his eyes, to feel his breath, to press my windpipe against his grip—After all I have endured, after all I have imagined, this is one of the most satisfying ways I can see to go. This is a way that at least one question might get an answer.

Survivor, but probably not for long.

Tattoo of my sister's first initial, eventually to be inked but not yet necessary.

Tattoos, as reminders, as warnings, as expectations of loss.

The sound of a black bag being zippered shut.

The sound of a brother comforting a brother, ignorant of the doom between them.

The sound of a bullet making wet music in his organs.

The sound of a car breaking the surface of a lake.

The sound of a confession, taped and played back.

The sound of a gunshot reverberating, echoing between concrete facades.

The sound of a knife, clacking against bone.

The sound of a message played over and over until the tape wears thin.

The sound of a phone going unanswered.

The sound of a police siren, of multiple sirens responding to multiple events.

The sound of a sentence heard three times, that means loss, that means murder, that means another taken from me.

The sound of a sister crying and crying.

The sound of a sister saying goodbye, saying that this will be the last time you will see her, for both your sakes.

The sound of a woman screaming for hours.

The sound of an alarm ringing.

The sound of sirens, a Doppler effect of passing emergency.

The sound of testimony, of witnessing.

The sound of words left unsaid.

Things that never were, and things that never will.

Understanding, as in lack thereof.

Vengeance, but never enough. Always state-sanctioned, always unsatisfying.

Victim is a broad term, a generalization, an umbrella under which we are all gathered at one time or another.

Violations of the law symbolize violations of the person, of the family, of the community. This is why they must be punished.

We regret to inform you.

We regret to inform you.

We regret to inform you.

What it takes to cut yourself off.

What it takes to defend your family.

What it takes to hide forever.

What it takes to kill a man.

What it takes to see this through to the end.

What it takes to solve the crime.

What it takes to take back what is yours.

Why, as in, Why us?

Witness, general.

Witnesses, specific: The other men and women who were with my father that night, plus the other people who were walking down the street when the shots were fired. The bartender and two waitresses, plus the policemen who arrived on the scene. I have interviewed them all myself, months later, after the conviction of the killer. The crime already solved, but not yet understood.

Wound, as in bullet hole, as in burn, as in puncture, as in slashing, as in fatal.

X, as in, to solve for X, as in, to complete the equation.

X, tattooed on my chest, above my heart.

X, that calls out to he who will commit this deed, to she who might end all that I am.

X, that marks the spot.

X, that will come to be.

X, which could stand for absolutely anything.

Y, the shape of an autopsy scar zippering the chest of a loved one.

Y, the sound of the question I cannot answer.

Y, the sound of the only question worth asking.

You, reading this.

You. Yes, you.

You, you, and you. You may not know yet, or maybe you always have, have felt the fist of the deed clenched in your heart for years. Please, do not wait any longer. I am tired of the fear, tired of the anticipation, tired of the day after day after day.

Zero, as brother.

Zero, as father.

Zero, as identity.

Zero, as memory.

Zero, as mother.

Zero, as name.

Zero, as self.

Zero, as silence.

Zero, as sister.

Zero: What will remain.

| ACKNOWLEDGEMENTS |

Thank you to the editors who first published these stories, including Ken Baumann, Sean Bishop, Laurie Cedilnik, Scott Garson, Roxane Gay, Aja Gabel, Sam Ligon, Steven J. McDermott, Bradford Morrow, Otto Penzler, M. Bartley Spiegel, and Beth Staples. A special thanks to Amanda Raczkowski, Joseph Reed, and Molly Gaudry for publishing my first two chapbooks, both of which are represented here in some form.

Thank you to the members of my various writing groups who served as the first readers and editors for these stories, including Aaron Burch, Blake Butler, Ryan Call, Elizabeth Ellen, Barry Graham, Sean Kilpatrick, Josh Maday, and Jeff Vande Zande.

Thank you to the many other writers who inspired and encouraged me, including Gary Amdahl, Suzanne Burns, Kim Chinquee, Dennis Cooper, Matthew Derby, Kitty Dubin, Brian Evenson, Tod Goldberg, Amelia Gray, Lily Hoang, Dave Housley, Laird Hunt, Charles Jensen, Michael Kimball, Norman Lock, Kyle Minor, Benjamin Percy, Jim Ruland, J.A. Tyler, Deb Olin Unferth, and William Walsh.

Thank you to my professors at Bowling Green State University, especially Michael Czyzniejewski and Wendell Mayo. Thanks also to the talented and inspiring friends I shared my years there with, especially Callista Buchen, Joe Celizic, Nikkita Cohoon, Dustin Hoffman, Brandon Jennings, Stephanie Marker, Catherine Templeton, Anne Valente, and Jacqueline Vogtman.

Thank you to Steven Gillis and Dan Wickett, for letting me work beside them at Dzanc Books. Thanks also to Tyler Gobble, Liana Imam, Matthew Olzmann,

Marie Schutt, Steven Seighman, and everyone else who works with me on *The Collagist* and *Best of the Web*.

Thank you to Peter Cole, for his long belief in these pages.

Thank you to my friends and family, especially my brothers Nick and Luke, my sisters Liz and Katie, and my parents Ken and Michele.

Thank you to everyone else I have neglected to thank in this too-small space: Your contributions and friendship have not gone forgotten or unappreciated.

Most importantly: Thank you to my wife Jessica, without whose constant love and support and friendship the making of these words would not have been possible.

Matt Bell's fiction has appeared in *Conjunctions,* *Hayden's Ferry Review,* *Willow Springs,* *Unsaid,* and *American Short Fiction,* and has been selected for inclusion in *Best American Mystery Stories 2010* and *Best American Fantasy 2.* He is the editor of *The Collagist* and can be found online at www.mdbell.com.